Strings

a love story

IMBRIFEX.

Also by
Megan Edwards

Getting Off on Frank Sinatra

Roads from the Ashes

Strings

a love story

Megan Edwards

IMBRIFEX BOOKS

IMBRIFEX BOOKS
Published by Flattop Productions, Inc.
8275 S. Eastern Avenue, Suite 200
Las Vegas, NV 89123

IMBRIFEX.

IMBRIFEX® is a registered trademark of Flattop Productions, Inc.

Printed in the United States of America.

Set in Adobe Caslon, Designed by Jennifer Heuer
Cover design by Jennifer Heuer and Suzanne Campbell

MeganEdwards.com
Imbrifex.com

ISBN 9781945501036 (trade paper)
ISBN 9781945501043 (e-book)
ISBN 9781945501067 (audiobook)

First Edition: September 2017
Library of Congress Control Number: 2017932680

For Margaret and Diana

Strings

a love story

Chapter 1

The Merino Rose is sitting on my coffee table. I can see it in the lights I left blazing in the practice room, but seeing it doesn't make it any more believable.

What's even more incredible is that the Merino Rose—"the violin of angels"—is actually mine. The Brahms Violin Concerto was played for the first time on this violin.

The King of Strings.

And it doesn't even exist. The Merino Rose was destroyed in the Trieste Opera fire in 1881. Everybody knows that. If a Guarnerius with inlaid roses around the back edge shows up at auction, it's got to be a fake.

Except—maybe not. What keeps those forgeries coming is that no one can prove that the fire destroyed the Merino Rose. No one can even prove the violin was actually in Trieste. It was Vittorio Bonacci who was there. Was the Merino Rose with him? Was he the thief who stole it from Joseph Joachim's Berlin conservatory?

The questions don't matter anymore. The violin is real. It's been gone for more than a century, and it vanished before reliable sound recording was invented. Even so, the legend of the Rose's unsurpassed brilliance has lived on. It defies reason, but the world still mourns the loss of a violin no one alive has ever heard.

I knew this was the Rose the instant I heard that one note. Yes, I have years of experience playing and appraising stringed instruments, but that knowledge only served to corroborate what I knew the moment I plucked that string. The Merino Rose is more than a haunting memory. The world will soon find out that one of its loveliest treasures still occupies three dimensions.

I can already see the cameras, the microphones, the throngs of reporters. When I say the word, they'll be here, each one more eager than the last to hear the edict of Edward Spencer IV. They consider me an undisputed authority, after all, an expert with unimpeachable credentials to give them the answer to the one question they're all dying to ask.

Oh, they'll listen in rapt silence while I play the Brahms, and they'll pretend they care when I speak of the Rose's sweet perfection. But that's not what they're really after. All they want is a number.

In the end I'll give them exactly that, and they'll go away happy, believing I have priced the priceless. They will never know what it really cost to bring the Merino Rose to my coffee table. Only Olivia knows, and she's not here.

I discovered I was a string man when I was eight years old and attending summer camp in Idaho. The music counselor handed me a violin when I arrived, and the moment I felt the smooth wood under my fingers, I was smitten.

At first, it was the construction of the thing that captivated me. I come from a manufacturing family—yes, I'm a Spencer from the Spencer Luggage family—and I'd spent my early years hearing about the intricacies of design and fabrication. I'd hung around our factory in Los Angeles every day after school, and I could have constructed a suitcase single-handed by the time I'd finished fourth grade. The violin was far finer than a valise, and its curved surfaces fascinated me. Even the bow seemed like a work of art.

If you think it odd that I'd never touched a violin until I was eight, you've never met my father. Edward Spencer III thought music was fine, in its place. He'd sung with the Yale Alley Cats when he was in college, but that was over once the sheepskin traded hands. Singing was just wholesome recreation, the same as summer camp. There was no room for it in real life. Hobbies like building models belonged there—that was practical engineering. But music? Frank Sinatra on the hi-fi while you sipped your pre-dinner Scotch—that was where music belonged.

Fathers, however, have always had a hard time stifling their children's infatuations. I was in love with the violin from that first moment of contact, and I spent the summer making it mine. The music counselor, happy to find an avid pupil, spent hours with me, got me excused from canoeing and archery. By the end of the summer, I could play.

And play I did. When my parents came to collect me on the last day of camp, I was the star of the talent show, the centerpiece of a group that included the music counselor and two of his friends who were members of the Spokane Symphony.

My parents were very proud, and they seemed to listen carefully when the music counselor told them I was a "natural talent."

"He should have lessons," Mike said, and he gave them the name of a teacher in Los Angeles.

My mother agreed that I should continue studying violin, and she arranged for lessons with Howard Stiles, who had just retired as concertmaster with the Los Angeles Philharmonic. Mr. Stiles wasn't the name my counselor had suggested. My mother moved in Los Angeles's social stratosphere, and if her son was going to study violin, the teacher would have to be Someone.

My father didn't start worrying about my love affair with music until I entered high school. I enrolled at Haviland, a boarding school located in the picturesque hamlet of Ojai in the oak-studded hills near Santa Barbara. The first three Edward Spencers had gone to Andover, but my father had decided when I was very young that if we were going to be a West Coast family, we needed to start some West Coast traditions. These new traditions didn't extend past high school, however. I'd known since I started eating solid food that I was expected to graduate from Yale.

For the first three years I attended Haviland, I played in the orchestra. This meant several performances each semester, and the big event was always the spring musical. I played for *Oklahoma!* and *The Music Man*, but the closest I ever came to acting was the title role in *Fiddler on the Roof.* It never crossed my mind to audition for a speaking part in one of these productions until my senior year. I happened to be standing near the music department office when Mr. Harper emerged and posted a flyer on the bulletin board.

"Auditions for all roles in *Camelot* will begin Tuesday, January 16, in Goddard Hall at four o'clock," the flyer read. I would have thought no more about it if Bill Cross hadn't read the words aloud.

"All roles except Lancelot," he continued as though he were still reading. "No tryouts are necessary for a role custom made for Haviland's pride, Ted Spencer."

Andy Beecham and a few other guys were standing nearby, and they all hooted. I felt color rise in my cheeks, and I couldn't stop myself from tossing my chemistry book into a hedge and tackling my best friend. Caught completely off guard, Bill landed in the hedge, too.

"Hey, this thing has thorns," he yelped. "Damn you, Spencer. I was only joking."

"Sorry," I said, grabbing his hand and helping him up. "Don't know what got into me."

"Good thing he didn't have his lance with him," Andy said, and all the guys laughed again.

"Screw you," I said, just as Mr. Harper stuck his head out the door.

"What's going on out here?" he asked.

"Nothing," Bill said quickly. "I just tripped, and Ted was just helping me up."

Mr. Harper heaved a weary sigh.

"Get moving," he said. "I know you all have someplace to be."

"Hey, come on. Just do it," Bill said as we headed toward the science building. "I'm stuck doing the lights. Harper says I have to train my replacements—a couple of freshmen."

"Ha," I said. "If he only knew what they're really going to learn."

Bill had been Haviland's light man since ninth grade. The light booth in Goddard Hall was his secret hideaway. Fortunately, he was very talented at snowing faculty members, or he would have been expelled many times over for what he did and stored in there.

"The key to doing anything you want," he used to say, "is remembering that what you are and what you seem don't have to match."

I envied him that. I could never seem like anything different from what I was, a self-consciously square violin player. Bill was a chameleon. To the Haviland faculty, he was a valuable asset. Not only did he keep the antiquated wiring system in Goddard Hall working flawlessly, he once prevented a fire in the science building by noticing a leaky gas valve in the chemistry lab. Another time, he saw that the retaining wall above the gym was developing a big crack. It turned out a water pipe had broken, and he was credited with saving the gym from a giant mudslide. Deeds like that are unusual for a high school student, and they gave Bill an equally unusual invincibility.

"You have to admit you'd make a good Lancelot," Bill went on. He dodged as I took another half-hearted swing at him. "No, Ted. I mean it. Good legs, golden curls, and we've all heard you in the shower. Perfect pitch."

"The hell with you, Cross," I said. Mr. Gillespie was standing at the door of the chemistry lab, or Bill might well have found himself in another hedge.

But Bill was right. Again. The guy was a master at pushing my buttons. If it hadn't been for him, I never would have joined the tennis team, and I would have gone my entire high school career without once drinking beer or sneaking off campus. I wasn't nearly appreciative enough at the time, but if it weren't for Bill, I would have been an impossible goody-goody.

Which, of course, was exactly why I was such a good candidate for the role of Lancelot. Even though I detested the idea at first, I couldn't help considering it. For starters, I actually had a little free time. Teachers know better than to try to get second-semester seniors to work very hard, and my college applications were in. Until the deciding envelopes arrived, I was in a tense holding pattern, and I longed for a little distraction. Gradually, I decided that an acting part in *Camelot* might be an amusing way to close out my four years at Haviland, and more chances to hang out with Bill in the light booth didn't sound too bad, either.

And so it came to pass that on the appointed day, I arrived at the back door of Goddard Hall at precisely four o'clock. I was not carrying a violin.

Chapter 2

I was a shoo-in for the role of Lancelot, but it wasn't because I was a fantastic actor. Only five boys showed up at the first round of tryouts, and *Camelot* has five significant male roles. Mr. Harper gave the part of Merlyn to Jonathan Griffith, who was the shortest among us, and the part of the aged King Pellinore to Greg Hornsby, who was skinny and not much taller. David Cummins, a pudgy bookworm type, got the role of Mordred. That left Arthur and Lancelot, and as soon as Mr. Harper told Brian Collier he'd have to work on his regal bearing, I knew Bill's prediction had been accurate. Even though I was happy about it by then, I was glad my buddy wasn't there. One smug smirk, and I would have decked him.

If casting the boys was easy for Mr. Harper, dealing with the girls more than made up for it. There was only one significant female role, and it seemed like every girl in school was determined to have it. "Who's going to be Guenevere?" echoed across the campus for days. The scuttlebutt around the dorms was that Elizabeth Dunhill would get the part. Not only was her father the president of Twentieth Century-Fox, he was a member of Haviland's board of trustees. How could Mr. Harper ignore those connections? If not Elizabeth, then Robin McCullough. Her father was the American ambassador to

Japan, and Robin had been acting in Haviland musicals since ninth grade. This was her last chance to be a star. And then there was Penelope Lambros, and Margaret Kellerman. Or what about Roberta Phillips? The list went on, and so did the midnight gossip sessions. It seemed unfair that I had walked into my own role so easily, but there was nothing to do but wait and see what decision emerged from Mr. Harper's office.

Olivia de la Vega. The group that had gathered around the bulletin board next to the music room looked at the name in disbelief. Two girls started to cry, and two more ran away. Brian and I, who had been inside Mr. Harper's office when he said he was ready to post his decision about Guenevere, just stared in surprise. Who the heck was Olivia de la Vega? Haviland was not a large school, and I was sure I knew everyone. But Olivia de la Vega? The name was new to me.

"Who—?" I began, but Brian interrupted.

"She's the daughter of one of the cleaning ladies," he said. "A sophomore."

Word spread like lightning, and the reaction was just as swift. Robin McCullough threw a noisy tantrum in the dining hall at lunch, and Elizabeth Dunhill swore she'd get Mr. Harper fired. I decided to keep a low profile until the hysteria blew over.

In spite of Robin's histrionics and Elizabeth's threats, rehearsals began on schedule. Mr. Harper, who no doubt had weathered some brutal telephone calls from parents and board members, didn't back down. Olivia de la Vega was Guenevere, and the Haviland student body would have to learn to live with it.

I didn't meet Olivia until the first rehearsal. It was a table reading of the script, and we were meeting in a conference room next to Goddard Hall. I was late, and the reading had already begun when I got there.

Olivia was speaking when I opened the door, and she paused to look up at me before continuing. Light from the window lit her face, and as our eyes met, I saw that hers were green. As she looked at me, the rest of the room fell away. A current as tangible as physical touch passed between us, and a shiver rippled through my body.

Olivia looked back down at her script, and I slid into a chair next to Jonathan Griffith. Mr. Harper shot me a disapproving glance over his reading glasses from the end of the table, but I hardly noticed. I was still under the spell of Olivia's gaze.

I sat there transfixed, unable to take my eyes off her as she read her lines. How could it be that I had not noticed her before? She was strikingly beautiful. She had long, smooth black hair and creamy skin that glowed golden in the afternoon sun. Her voice sounded as if she were singing even though she wasn't, and she used her hands when she spoke. They were lovely, delicate hands, with slender fingers that seemed almost translucent. And those eyes. Those marvelous, magical green eyes.

Jonathan nudged me under the table, yanking me from my thoughts. "Who'd've thought we'd get a Mexican Guenevere?" he whispered.

"Shut up," I said.

Mr. Harper had won his skirmish, and my leading lady had won her role. But the battle for Camelot had barely begun.

Chapter 3

God, it was a battle. It was actually fortunate for Olivia that she didn't live in the girls' dorm. She and her mother, the housekeeper for said dorm, shared a little stucco cottage behind the maintenance building. Haviland had a policy that the children of full-time employees, even the janitors and kitchen help, could attend the school gratis if they could meet admission requirements. Though it was a generous benefit, it extended only to tuition, not to a room in a dormitory. Since most of the eligible offspring were already housed on campus with their parents, it made sense from a financial point of view. The trouble was, social interaction at Haviland happened mostly in the dorms, which meant that the children of employees were mostly excluded. The teachers' children, who possessed enough confidence to climb through windows at night, suffered the least, but kids like Olivia were so invisible they weren't even shunned. If she hadn't tried out for the musical, I might well have graduated without knowing Olivia existed.

But she did try out, even though her mother, I later learned, tried her best to talk her out of it.

"Don't torture yourself, Livie," she'd said when Olivia announced her plan. "You don't have a chance against all those debutantes."

Eleanor de la Vega later told me herself that she knew her warning was futile.

"When Olivia makes her mind up," she said, shaking her head, "forty mules can't budge her. But I thought it was worth a try."

A nasty little editorial in the school paper aroused my wrath. It appeared the day after Mr. Harper announced his decision. "Taco Time in Camelot," the headline read, and even though it was against school rules to publish a story anonymously, the piece was mysteriously byline-free.

I knew who'd written it the second I saw it. Elizabeth Dunhill was the editor of the *Haviland Horn*, and she'd recently whipped up a tempest with another of her little masterpieces: a detailed article about how to grow, store, and smoke marijuana in a dorm room without getting caught. In 1968, it was enough to convene an emergency meeting of the board of trustees. Elizabeth, in exchange for agreeing not to submit the story to a local paper, got off with a warning, and the next day, she wore pajamas to her American history class to protest the school's uniform requirements. I mention the latter incident to illustrate the fact that Elizabeth was not driven by principle. She just liked making a splash, and she took advantage of the immunity her powerful father gave her.

Elizabeth wasn't unique. Most students at Haviland had been guilty of such entitled behavior at one time or another. Prep schools strive to maintain high standards and strict codes of conduct, but they can't afford to bite the hands that pay for their science buildings. Elizabeth was attached to one of those hands. Still, I couldn't accept the possibility that there might well be no penalty for her cruel diatribe against Olivia. If things took their accustomed course, the headmaster would give a terse little talk in morning assembly on his favorite theme: *To whom much is given, much is expected*. If I didn't do something, that would be the end of it.

For the first time in my own overprivileged experience, I personally felt the sting of injustice. Olivia was so damned innocent, and she seemed so powerless to defend herself. I had never met anyone so obviously in need of a champion, and I had already been given the title. I was Lancelot, and Elizabeth Dunhill's editorial spurred me to action.

I didn't wait for Dr. Whitehead's morning sermon. I was too full of righteous anger, especially when it became apparent that the majority of Haviland's student body didn't care a bit about Elizabeth's racist remarks. After my history class let out, I headed straight for the headmaster's office. I'd be late for rehearsal, but this was too important to put on hold.

Christopher Whitehead was the quintessential prep school leader, imported directly from the land of school ties and A levels. He had all the right credentials, including an accent that would make Queen Elizabeth weep with pride. On the wall behind his desk hung his Oxford diploma and a triumphal oar from his sculling days at Balliol.

Fortunately, he wasn't an over-gentrified fop. In fact, he was a pretty good guy, and he was succeeding remarkably well guiding Haviland through the rough waters of the Vietnam era. In the good old days of the Free Speech Movement, campus unrest was as much a fact of life at elitist prep schools as it was on college campuses.

If I had been a different person, Elizabeth's editorial might have inspired me to organize a sit-in or a noisy protest. But I was an apolitical violin player, and I wasn't into global causes. I had never marched into a headmaster's office unannounced before, and I could tell from Dr. Whitehead's expression that he was just as surprised as I was.

His secretary had already left for the day, and since the door to his study was half open, I just walked straight in without knocking. Dr.

Whitehead was standing with his back to the door, a wisp of smoke rising over his head. He appeared to be looking for a book on the shelf under his oar, and he didn't hear me enter. By way of announcement, I cleared my throat.

Dr. Whitehead spun around immediately. He removed the carved meerschaum pipe from between his lips and looked at me questioningly. He was a fairly young man to have his job, not exactly Mr. Chips. He couldn't have been much past forty, and his wavy brown hair was trendily cut in a style halfway between the Beatles and John Kennedy.

"Mr. Spencer!" he said, smiling. "Or should I say Lancelot? You sneaked up on me!"

"I'm sorry, sir. I should have knocked."

"No, no. The door was open." Dr. Whitehead tamped out his pipe and sat down in the leather swivel chair behind his desk. I sat down on the other side in one of the two upholstered chairs facing him. It had been quite a while since I'd been in his office. Dr. Whitehead was a hands-on, mingle-with-the-masses kind of leader. Usually if you went looking for him in his office, you wouldn't find him there.

"What can I do for you, Spencer?" Dr. Whitehead asked. He folded his hands on the blotter in front of him and waited.

"Well, I—" I couldn't believe it. I was stammering, and I couldn't seem to help myself. "I—I'm really upset about the editorial in today's *Horn*."

"Oh." Dr. Whitehead paused, then extracted a copy of the paper from a folder on his desk. "I, too, found the piece upsetting." He paused again, and I rushed to fill the silence.

"It's—it's racism at its worst!" I blurted. "And we all know who wrote it! She should be expelled!"

Dr. Whitehead took his time before responding to my outburst.

He looked at the paper, perused the story again. I wondered how many other people had already bent his ear about it.

"As I'm sure you're aware, Mr. Spencer," he said at last, "we do not know positively who the author is. But whoever wrote it, Mr. Kincaid should never have let it run."

Mr. Kincaid was the *Horn*'s faculty adviser, and my wrath was rekindled as I realized he was going to be the fall guy.

"Elizabeth Dunhill wrote it!" I almost shouted. "Everyone knows it! She's been boasting all day!"

Dr. Whitehead was maddening in his measured response, and I was tempted to grab his oar off the wall behind him and whack him with it.

"Calm down, Spencer," he said. Another pause as he pushed up his wire-rims and looked me straight in the eye. "Perhaps you will enlighten me as to why you are making this your personal crusade."

I jumped to my feet. "It should be everyone's crusade!" I cried. "Olivia de la Vega's civil rights have been violated! Isn't this what Selma was for? Isn't this what Martin Luther King is always talking about?"

Once again, Dr. Whitehead was infuriatingly slow in his response, and I sank back into the chair with my head down, fuming. My heart was racing, and I could feel beads of sweat collecting on my forehead. Why *was* I so upset, anyway?

I looked up, locked eyes once again with the headmaster, and suddenly, I knew. What's worse, Christopher Whitehead knew, too. I had just made a giant horse's ass of myself.

Chapter 4

As I stumbled out of Dr. Whitehead's office, the full realization of my affliction washed over me. I was in a state of full-blown puppy love, a condition I had naively misidentified as genuine humanitarian concern. But how was I supposed to know? Somehow, in my seventeen years on earth, I had never developed a crush on a girl before. I hadn't even dated, unless you count a couple of debutantes my mother had insisted I escort to their coming-out balls. Five hours of violin practice every day didn't leave time for much beyond academics and sleep. I was a virgin in every way possible.

This is the story I've been telling myself for the last thirty-three years. Acknowledging the real nature of my connection with Olivia would have been far too painful. Instead, I've convinced myself I was an innocent boy, caught in the hot flush of infatuation. It happens to everyone, doesn't it, that overwhelmingly powerful tsunami of emotion that vanishes almost as abruptly as it arrives? It was just a crush, a youthful, desperate obsession. It must have been! How could it possibly have been anything else? There's no such thing as love at first sight, and children aren't capable of lasting feelings. Right?

I've always known I was lying to myself. I've let my mind do all the talking, and I've persuaded my heart to stay mute. It's an uneasy truce that might have lasted the rest of my life if Olivia hadn't rolled up my driveway yesterday.

It's been over three decades since our eyes first met in a schoolroom on a January afternoon, but when I opened my front door to find her smiling there, not a single moment had elapsed. Her eyes met mine, and my heart pounded the truth it had always held. Olivia and I share a link that time cannot corrode, that distance cannot sever.

How can she be gone again? How can I live without her? I can't even retreat into denial with this violin here to remind me. I know I could tuck it away in a cabinet, but I can't bring myself to move it beyond my sight. Like a moth drawn to a lighted candle, I somehow need to suffer its silent accusations. No matter how painful, never again will I try to ignore my love for Olivia.

I couldn't have ignored it even if I had tried back then in high school. During *Camelot* rehearsals, I wasn't acting. When I sang "If Ever I Would Leave You" to Olivia, I meant every word about how I could never do it. And of course I had to kiss her, which terrified me until I found out that touching lips with someone who is only acting doesn't mean much. Even so, it inspired vivid dreams when I was off stage.

Haviland's founder had been a firm believer in personal space, which meant that every boarder had a private room. I know that sounds cushy, but the rooms were little more than walk-in closets. There was barely enough space for a twin bed, a desk, and a small wardrobe. Nonetheless, I was grateful for that cubicle of solitude, especially those last few months in residence. In my room, I could dream of Olivia without embarrassment, and I retreated there so often that my friends began wondering what was wrong with me.

"What's with you, man?" Bill Cross asked one afternoon after he'd burst into my room unannounced. He parked himself on my bed and tore open a bag of M&M's. "It's like you've become a monk or something."

"I have not," I replied as nonchalantly as possible. "I just have too much to do. Thanks to you and Lancelot."

"Ha!" Bill said. "You know you love it." He dumped a pile of M&M's onto my pillow and started picking out all the green ones. "So what's the deal?"

"I—I'm worried about college," I said. "I haven't heard anything yet."

Bill threw a handful of M&M's at me.

"Cut it out, slob," I said. "I always get ants after you've been in here."

"Tell me the truth."

"I did."

Bill jumped up and thumped me on the chest. "Bullshit. Bullshit. Bullshit," he said, and he ran out and slammed the door before I could do anything to retaliate.

In fact, I hadn't told Bill a total lie. I actually *was* worried about college, which is another excuse I've used all these years to justify my behavior toward Olivia. I had known my whole life that I was expected to enroll at Yale, but Albert van Doren, the Santa Barbara violinist with whom I'd studied since ninth grade, had infected me with the notion of attending the Juilliard School. He had helped me with my application, and he had even agreed to travel with me to New York for my audition. My father thought the whole idea was ridiculous, but my mother convinced him to humor me. Neither one believed that I was really good enough on the violin to be offered a spot at Juilliard, and I was a shoo-in at Yale. Why not let me choose my own backup school?

I was grateful for their indulgence because I knew in my belly I could never follow the well-marked trail of my forebears. I would never major in economics and join the coterie around the boardroom table at Spencer Luggage, Inc. The only luggage I wanted anything to do with was a violin case.

The trouble lay in the possibility that I'd score acceptances from both institutions. I've always done my best to avoid confrontations. As a child, when I knew we were having lima beans for dinner, I would wear a sweatshirt with a pouch to the table. The offending food would disappear, and my mother was never the wiser. I could deal with, "Ted! Aren't you hot in that sweatshirt?" better than I could handle a face-off about the real issue.

Even though I wasn't sure I'd be accepted to Juilliard, I prayed for a rejection letter from Yale. Of course, with the illustrious careers of three Edward Spencers paving a golden road ahead of me, I might as well have hoped for the earth to change course. I had the inexorable force of legacy combined with a near-perfect grade point average to guarantee a "yes" letter from New Haven.

If I got into Juilliard, a showdown with my parents would be inevitable, and I awaited my April envelopes with a feeling of foreboding. Thoughts of Olivia were even more intoxicating when they distracted me from playing out the unavoidable battle I was doomed to wage. I lived for *Camelot* rehearsals, and the rest of the time, I clung to the moments I'd spent with Olivia, weaving from them delicious new scenarios.

She really was incredible, and I'm not just talking about my feelings for her. From my earlier experiences with Haviland's spring musicals, I expected lots of fooling around at rehearsals. Mr. Harper's exasperated threats would steadily increase in number and intensity until opening night loomed so large that everybody had to learn their lines or risk terminal embarrassment. Once, when Tevye had missed his third *Fiddler* rehearsal in a row, Mr. Harper said, "Well, Ted, at least we'll have a decent fiddler up there on the roof. I swear, you're the only person here who really understands the importance of practicing."

At the first *Camelot* rehearsal, Mr. Harper made the whole cast sit in the front rows of the auditorium. Bill Cross and his two apprentices were in the booth at the back testing the stage lights, and as Mr. Harper delivered his pep talk over the whispers and snickers, the footlights behind him changed from blue to red to yellow.

"Okay," said Mr. Harper after he'd commanded us to learn our lines no later than the end of February, "we're going to begin with Guenevere's first number."

He punched the button on his tape recorder, and Olivia walked up on stage to the last strains of the overture. Penelope Lambros said, "Oh, my God" a little too loudly, and Caroline Buckley said something else that made all the girls laugh. They were still giggling when the overture ended.

When her number began, Olivia opened her mouth to sing. But before she could, somebody let out a loud, prolonged burp. It echoed all over the auditorium, and everyone froze. It was too awful, even for spoiled Haviland brats.

Mr. Harper stared at us, his face a ghastly yellow from a spotlight Bill was testing. He shook his head, and then he reached for the tape recorder. His finger was just descending to the "off" button when Olivia's voice filled the auditorium.

The yellow spotlight flicked off, and a white one suddenly lit up Olivia. As though nothing at all had happened, she kept on singing.

I was spellbound, but given my feelings for her, that wasn't surprising. What was astonishing is that everyone else was struck dumb, too. Olivia de la Vega, the invisible girl who lived in a cleaning lady's cottage, stood there singing as though she had been born in the foot-lights. Her voice left no room in Goddard Hall for anything but awe. The final notes of her song were still hanging in the air when Mr. Harper clicked off the tape recorder.

Olivia stood on the stage, the white spotlight full on her face. Everyone was quiet, even the girls in the front row. Then, from some-where in the back, came the sound of one person clapping. I turned, and, silhouetted in the light booth, I could see Bill Cross and the two freshmen. They started clapping, too, and one of them whistled. Then the spotlight followed Olivia as she walked off the stage, and the room fell silent again.

I wish I could say that from that moment on, everyone was friendly toward Olivia, but that didn't happen. The girls kept a surly distance, and the boys turned shy. But to Mr. Harper's great delight, our rehearsals were suddenly very serious affairs. Though they still snubbed her, the girls tried their damnedest to match Olivia's profes-sionalism on stage. The boys struggled, too, even though there was no hope we could look like anything but rank amateurs. It was a real miracle. All Olivia had done was sing her song, but it brought the best out in all of us.

Most importantly, it brought out the best in me. Because of her, I was a better Lancelot than I ever dreamed possible. Olivia maintained a flawlessly professional front, and I strove to match it. I memorized all my lines and lyrics within a week, and I practiced singing when I should have been playing my violin.

When I made it through a rehearsal, I'd retreat immediately to my room to let my feelings flood over me. Lying on my narrow bed, I would go back over every moment. I tried to feel her presence, to breathe her in. I relived every smile, every touch, every word.

The trouble was, the words were all courtesy of Lerner and Loewe.

Even after a month of rehearsals, Olivia and I still hadn't exchanged a sentence that wasn't in the script. Olivia was punctual at Goddard Hall every afternoon, and she departed when Mr. Harper gave the nod. In between, she was all business.

But, oh, when she was Guenevere! Those liquid green eyes bore straight into mine as she professed first her scorn and then her ever-lasting love. As I struggled to match her ability and strove to take direction as easily, I hoped desperately that my feelings might make up for my lack of acting experience. I have no doubt, however, that I looked exactly like what I was: an awkward high school kid in tights. At least Bill had been right about my voice. I could carry a tune, and my legs weren't bad.

At the end of February, I received a letter from Juilliard inviting me to come to New York for an audition. I couldn't quite believe it. It wasn't an offer of acceptance, but it was tangible encouragement. Damn! Even if I never got to go there as a student, I was definitely going to see it. I was going to walk through the door, try the place on for size. All at once, one of my dreams was tantalizingly close to coming true.

Riding on the wave of confidence this good news inspired, I decided to invite Olivia to go to the Spring Gala with me. The Spring Gala was Haviland's version of a prom, and every student in the school willing to pay the price of admission was invited. I'd never attended, and I was nearly positive Olivia hadn't either. Tickets were close to a hundred bucks a couple, which was a lot of money in 1968. The event was held at the Ojai Valley Hunt Club, a fancy resort not far from Haviland where my parents stayed when they came to visit.

I figured Olivia might accept my invitation just so she could go to the Gala. Since I was certain she harbored no feelings for me, my offer would really be a bribe, and I hoped desperately I was dealing in the right currency to tempt her.

I should admit that my plan held another advantage. Every year, my parents asked why I didn't go to the Gala.

"Social gatherings are an important part of success," my father would say, and my mother would agree. If I went to the dance, maybe things would go a little better when I announced that Juilliard was more than a pipe dream.

It took me nearly a week to strengthen my resolve. Lying on my bed, I rehearsed my lines a thousand times, and I even forced myself to consider the possibility Olivia might say no. The only reason she'd reject me, I supposed, was that she'd feel uncomfortable in a formal setting. She'd probably never been to a place like the Hunt Club before, I imagined. Since she might worry about what to wear, I even concocted a half-baked scheme to furnish her with a prom dress anonymously.

> *Dear Miss de la Vega,*
>
> *Congratulations! You are the lucky winner of a FREE PROM DRESS at Norm Taylor's State Street Boutique! Just stop by our Santa Barbara store to claim your ABSOLUTELY FREE, NO-OBLIGATION prize!*

I would have made a lousy fairy godmother, but as things turned out, it didn't matter. When I finally mustered enough gumption to pop the question, Olivia caught me by surprise.

We were alone when I asked her, an encounter that had required both planning and luck to accomplish. The teacher in charge of creating and acquiring all the costumes for *Camelot* made individual appointments with each of the lead actors. I'd checked the sign-up sheet to see when Olivia's meeting would take place, and at the appropriate time, I'd stationed myself outside the door through which I hoped she'd depart Goddard Hall. Luckily, my prediction was right, and even better, she was alone when she emerged.

Olivia saw me leaning oh-so-casually against a bougainvillea-shaded column along the walkway outside Goddard Hall, and she murmured a greeting but swept on past. I had to hurry to keep up with her as she walked purposefully away from me.

"Olivia! I'm glad I bumped into you."

Olivia paused, turned her green eyes on me for a moment, and then started walking again. I leapt ahead of her, turned, and walked backwards, facing her.

"Do you have a minute? I'd like to talk to you."

Olivia stopped abruptly and looked me square in the eyes. "Sure, Ted. What is it?"

By the grace of God, I didn't stammer. "I wanted to ask you if you'd like to go to the Spring Gala with me."

My words hung there as Olivia stared at me and then looked away. She paused long enough for both hope and despair to well up inside me, and then, without any emotion that I could read, she laid her three hideously simple words on me.

"No, thank you."

And that was it. She didn't offer any excuses or the slightest opening through which I might insert my practiced persuasions. *No, thank you,* and she was gone.

Chapter 5

I had never been more astonished and deflated at the same moment. When Olivia left me in the walkway, my mouth was gaping open. I don't remember making my way to my dorm room, but I do know I missed dinner that night. I lay on my bed and consumed an entire box of graham crackers in the gathering gloom.

All my daydreams of attending the dance with Olivia on my arm had been unceremoniously dashed, and she'd left me with no encouragement to try another tack. I was despondent for three days, and I missed four classes. Such absences would have aroused little comment had it not been for my otherwise perfect attendance record. When the school nurse summoned me to her office on the third day of my funk, I realized I was risking parental involvement.

I rallied enough not to miss any more school, but I still wallowed in my woe. *Camelot* rehearsals would have been particularly horrible, but fortuitously I was excused. Albert van Doren and I flew to New York for my audition at Juilliard that week.

I had never been to Manhattan before, and I know my mother was disappointed that she wasn't the one who would be showing it to me for the first time. She had worked in New York for a few years after she finished college, and she had planned to take me there as a graduation present.

"You still can," I said, "because I won't have time to sightsee on this trip. It'll be all business."

My mother laughed, because that was my father's line. Every time he took off for Hong Kong or Singapore, it was "all business."

I actually believed what I told my mother, but I couldn't have been more wrong. My time at the Juilliard School accounted for only a small fraction of the trip, and Mr. Van Doren, a former New Yorker himself, was eager to introduce me to the glories of Manhattan.

The first afternoon we were there, we took a walk in Central Park after we checked into the Warwick Hotel. It was February and bitingly cold, but I barely noticed. I was too entranced by the city I had, up to now, known only in story and song. Suddenly, here it all was, swirling around me like a painting that had magically come to life. Ladies in fur coats were walking little jacketed dogs while steam-breathing men sold chestnuts from pushcarts. Men wearing gloves with the fingers cut off made change for their customers at news kiosks and bookstands. A horse-drawn carriage passed right in front of me. A man and a woman wrapped in a plaid blanket were kissing in the back seat. The man had his hand on the back of the woman's neck, and I could see her fingers on his cheek. I stared at them, and, as powerfully as if someone had shoved me, an overwhelming resolve slammed through me. Someday, I swore as the carriage moved on, Olivia and I will be under a blanket just like that.

The thought repeated itself over and over as Mr. Van Doren and I dined at a restaurant overlooking the East River. We watched the lights on the Brooklyn Bridge and the city lights sparkling beyond.

"You'll do fine tomorrow, Ted," my teacher said as we finished up our steaks. "Just remember to stay in the music. Like it's a pocket of oxygen in outer space."

It was advice he had given me a thousand times before, but that night it only reminded me of Olivia. I was in New York at last, on my way to an audition at Juilliard, and all I could think of was getting back to boarding school and finding a way into her bubble.

I lay awake most of the night, telling myself in vain that I should sleep. I kept seeing myself with Olivia, riding in a carriage in Central Park, bundled tightly in a plaid blanket. And then it would be spring, and I would be playing my violin while she sat smiling on a bench. And everyone walking by would smile, too, and there would be daffodils and squirrels, and—I must have dozed off at some point, because I woke up when Mr. Van Doren knocked on my door.

Back then, I thought it was amazing that my audition went well, but now I know that it would have been far more surprising if it had gone badly. Not only was I well prepared, I had chosen a piece I considered my favorite at the time, Paganini's "Last Caprice in A Minor." That alone might not have been enough to guarantee a flawless performance, but Olivia was. I was playing for her that morning, and I could almost see her there, the one familiar face among all the strange, critical ones. Just as Mr. Van Doren had advised, I stayed in the music. What he couldn't have known was that Olivia had become my music. She is still my music. She is my pocket of oxygen in outer space.

Mr. Van Doren wasn't allowed to sit in on my audition, but a friend of his on the faculty called him before we left New York and said he had "a student to be proud of."

"It doesn't mean anything until you get the letter, Ted," Mr. Van Doren told me, "but David Krinsky didn't have to call. It's a very positive sign."

By the time we headed back to California, I had taken a ride on the Staten Island Ferry, toured the Metropolitan Museum of

Art, admired the view from the top of the Empire State Building, and attended a piano recital at Carnegie Hall. Through it all, I kept swearing to myself that somehow I'd get Olivia to talk to me.

When I returned to Haviland, however, I found I was still paralyzed by the thought of rejection and at a loss over what to do next. I was even considering the desperate step of confessing my feelings to Bill and enlisting his help. Then one Tuesday night, everything changed.

I was studying in the library. I had chosen a small table in a little alcove surrounded by bookcases. It was my favorite spot because it provided a little privacy, which meant I could get away with eating as I worked. I had just taken a big bite off a Snickers bar when I felt eyes upon me. Expecting to find the disapproving visage of the night librarian scowling at me, I yanked my contraband under the table and looked up.

Instead of a pair of horn-rimmed glasses, two green eyes met mine. It was Olivia.

"Hi, Ted," she said, smiling. "Don't worry. I won't tell."

My God. She was actually initiating a conversation with me. My heart took two beats at once, and I sucked in a breath that nearly caused me to choke on my candy bar.

"I was hoping I'd find you here." She paused, looked down, and then fixed her eyes on me again. I never stopped staring, and I can remember what she had on as if this all happened two hours ago. She was wearing faded jeans and a navy blue V-neck sweater. A delicate gold chain disappeared in a point between her breasts. Her smooth dark hair was drawn back in a loose ponytail, and she was carrying a spiral notebook and a beat-up copy of *The Grapes of Wrath*. I'd never seen her in anything except a school uniform before, and she seemed infinitely more beautiful, fascinating, and unattainable than ever.

"I wanted to ask you if you'd like to go to a music festival with me."

I must have maintained my silence a bit too long, because Olivia continued before I could respond.

"My mother is performing at the folk music festival in Santa Barbara this weekend—near the university. She plays Celtic harp, and—"

I was still dumbfounded.

"Well, if you want to go, we could—"

"I'd love to," I finally managed to interject. A brief but awkward silence ensued, and I struggled to say something that wouldn't sound too stupid.

"Your mother plays the harp?"

"Celtic harp," corrected Olivia. "It's her Irish roots, I guess, but anyway, she's really good, and she plays every year at this thing. It's kind of a Renaissance fair. A lot of people wear costumes."

Another awkward pause.

"But we wouldn't have to."

"This weekend?"

"Yes, both days, but I was thinking we could go on Saturday. Unless—"

"Saturday's fine."

Olivia hung around for a couple more minutes while we worked out the logistics. I would have liked her to stay all evening, but as soon as we'd arranged to meet in the gym parking lot at nine o'clock Saturday morning, she picked up her books.

"Bye, Ted," she said, and she vanished before I could think of anything to delay her.

I stared after her, my mood already rising to euphoria. A three-minute conversation and I was a changed man. Olivia had not only talked to me, she had actually invited me to go somewhere with her. For a whole day. God!

There were three *Camelot* rehearsals between the night Olivia invited me to the festival and Saturday morning, but my hopes for talking to her further were annihilated at the first one. Olivia was still all business when it came to acting, and she maintained her usual distance, even during breaks. Had she really asked me out? I felt as if I'd imagined our library rendezvous, but the only way I'd find out for sure was to show up Saturday morning at the parking lot next to the gym.

I will never forget the days leading up to my date with Olivia. They were filled with more intense anticipation than any I've spent before or since. I was far less nervous before my audition for the Vienna Philharmonic Orchestra. I had fewer jitters before my first performance in Carnegie Hall. I worried about everything: my haircut, my aftershave, a pimple that was burgeoning on the side of my nose.

On Friday night I was fretting about what slacks to wear when Bill Cross caught me in the highly uncharacteristic act of ironing a madras shirt in the dorm laundry room.

"Lancelot's got a hot date with Guenevere, I see," he commented with his signature sarcasm, and I couldn't muster a quick enough rejoinder.

"Oh, my God," continued Bill when he saw the deer-caught-in-the-headlights look on my face. "You really are going out with her?"

I didn't have to answer. Bill rushed up and grabbed the iron out of my hand.

"Hey, watch out!" I yelled. "It's on the cotton setting!"

"Shut up and sit down," Bill said. "You don't know what you're doing, anyway. I'll iron. You talk."

I gave up and flopped down on a folding chair next to the dryer.

"You're looking at someone who spent his formative years under the guidance of one of the world's greatest laundresses," Bill said. He was referring to his early childhood in Venezuela, where his father was still in the oil business. Bill lived there until he was nine, when his parents split up, and he came to the States with his mother. Both parents had remarried and had more children, which meant that Bill was a half brother to three girls and two boys, all much younger. Bill sometimes referred to himself as "the early mistake," and I always had the feeling that he hadn't come up with the term himself.

"Yeah," he continued, "I got two things from growing up at the knee of Maria del Pilar Mata de Salazar. Accent-free Spanish and a mighty skill with starch." He turned the collar on my shirt. "This could actually use a little, but you're already too stiff." Bill gave me a look, and I knew I had to start talking.

"She invited me," I said.

"Interesting," Bill said. "I could have sworn it was you doing all the pining away."

God, had I been that obvious?

"So where are you going?" Bill asked.

"A folk music festival," I said.

"Your idea?" Bill said, surprised.

"Hers."

"Hmm. How're you getting there?"

"Her mom's driving," I said. There it all was, ready for voracious consumption in the dorms. The violin virtuoso was going to a love-in with the cleaning lady and her daughter. There was nothing to stop Bill from spreading the word.

I've never admitted to myself until now that I was worried about my reputation there in the laundry room. I had relished the thought of showing up at the Spring Gala with Guenevere on my arm. I would have loved to parade her in front of Elizabeth Dunhill and her snotty society cronies. Olivia would have been my trophy at the Ojai Valley Hunt Club, but a trip to a folk music festival with her—a place where they played things like spoons and kazoos—was something else entirely. It was exactly the sort of event my classical training had taught me to scorn.

"Here's your shirt," Bill said. "Say thanks."

I took the shirt.

"Say thanks," Bill said again, but I left without a word. I figured it was only a matter of hours before the entire campus would be laughing as I rode off to hear banjo music in a ratty old Chevy station wagon.

But Bill didn't spread the word about my plans. I'm not sure whether it was because he was my friend or that he considered Olivia's feelings, but either way, his silence made him a better man than I. As I headed back to my room to decide which pair of slacks to wear, I was nothing more than a chicken-hearted snob who was terrified his classmates might find out that he was about to embark on his first real date.

Chapter 6

Whenever I size up new locales, it's always Santa Barbara I use as a measuring stick. Nowhere on the California coast has architecture wedded its setting with such seductive perfection. White adobe and terra cotta tile mingle with the dark green spires of ancient cedars. The city slopes gently down to its world-famous coastline, where miles of sugar-white beaches greet the rolling turquoise surf. Balmy ocean breezes bear the scent of jasmine and honeysuckle almost every day of the year. In spring, the whole place erupts in an ecstatic explosion of fuchsias, begonias, roses, bougainvillea, and geraniums.

Ever since my four years at Haviland, no matter where I've lived, I have always cultivated at least one geranium in a red clay pot to remind me of that riotous California springtime. When denizens of less temperate zones assail me with long-winded speeches about how they could never live in a place that has no seasons, I never try to set them straight. I just look at my geranium and remember rebirth on the Western edge. I remember Santa Barbara and being seventeen. I remember Olivia.

On Saturday, I got up at four to practice my violin, then stationed myself on a terrace next to the science building at eight thirty. I could see the gym from my vantage point, and my plan was to wait until I saw the station wagon pull into the parking lot. Then I'd saunter on down in a fashion I desperately hoped would come across as casual. Unfortunately, Mr. Gillespie was working early in his lab, and he saw me through the side window. He immediately joined me on the terrace.

"Spencer!" he called jovially as he emerged from the building. "What brings you to science land so early on a Saturday?"

I could tell that Mr. Gillespie, whom I actually liked a lot, was in a mood to chat.

"Oh, uh—"

"I think I've finally convinced Puck to stop barking at the orchestra," Mr. G. continued. "Now all we have to worry about is the audience." Puck, Mr. Gillespie's sheepdog, had the role of King Pellinore's shaggy companion in *Camelot*. His looks made him perfect for the part, but his personality was making things difficult.

"I'm sure he'll be fine," I replied, still wondering how I could escape and find a better place to count down to nine o'clock in private.

"Well," said Mr. G. heartily, "at least we've got the perfect Lancelot." He clapped me on the back.

"Sir—I've got to go. I've got an appointment," I blurted. With Mr. Gillespie staring after me, I took off down the stone steps to the path below. I was still trotting when I turned right onto the one-lane road that led to the gym parking lot and heard a car closing in behind me. I jumped over the curb and turned to see Olivia and her mother laughing behind a dusty windshield. I smiled lamely. So much for looking casual. Olivia stepped out, opened the back door, and disappeared inside.

"You ride in front!" she called, leaning out of the window. "Your legs are longer than mine!"

I slid onto the peeling vinyl and pulled the door shut. The car smelled of incense, and a string of glass beads swung from the rear-view mirror.

"Hello, Mrs. de la Vega," I said. "Thank you for inviting me to come along today."

"You can call me Eleanor unless it makes you feel uncomfortable, Ted," she replied. "And you're welcome, but you really have to thank Olivia. It was all her idea."

I twisted my head around. "Thank you, Olivia," I said. Olivia smiled her response from the back seat.

Both Eleanor and Olivia were wearing long dresses. Eleanor's was a Shakespearean-style gown with a tight bodice that pushed her breasts up and gave her eye-catching cleavage. I tried not to stare at her as she drove but, until that morning, I had never seen her in anything except a brown housekeeper's uniform that made her look at least two decades older than she was. I hadn't been able to picture her as a performer, but now, with her hair attractively styled and her face made up with professional skill, I could no longer imagine her mopping floors. Like her daughter, she was beautiful. She had the same delicate fingers, I noted as I watched her navigate the curving road down the hill. Her hair was lighter, and she had freckles, but her green eyes were the same shade as Olivia's. And they laughed the same, a bubbly giggle that made me laugh, too.

Olivia's dress wasn't a costume. It was made of something white and gauzy, and the bodice was much more modest than Eleanor's. Olivia was wearing a wreath of flowers in her hair, and the whole effect was delightfully Botticellian. The two of them made me feel terminally un-hip. My plaid madras shirt and khaki slacks might have been considered "cool" at my parents' tennis club, but in the current context I felt like a charter member of the Young Republicans. If you don't remember the sixties, that was a designation far worse than "nerd." At least I didn't sport a crew cut, and I had, at the last minute, decided to wear sandals.

I couldn't worry about my wardrobe for long. Eleanor and Olivia were too busy laughing and making plans for me to feel self-conscious.

"I'll be playing all day, Ted," said Eleanor. "You and Olivia will be on your own until six or so. How long did you sign out for?"

Haviland required that all boarding students "sign out" when they left campus, which was only allowed on weekends and, if you were a senior with decent grades, a couple of evenings during the week. Students weren't allowed to keep cars on campus, which, given the isolated location of the school, seriously limited your travel options unless you had local friends.

"I said I'd be back around nine."

"Oh, good! That'll give us time for dinner! Can we go to Carmen's, Mom?" Olivia's obvious enthusiasm for making the day last as long as possible lifted my spirits.

"We'll see, Livie," replied Eleanor. "We'll just play things by ear."

After four days of planning and worrying, I liked the idea of just letting things unfold. I liked Eleanor, too, and the psychedelic peace symbol stuck to her dashboard. I liked riding through the orange groves along Highway 150, and I liked that Olivia was humming as we drove. Our sweet and happy journey brought us at last to Isla Vista Park, where a jolly crowd was gathering and music was already rising over the lawns that sloped down to the sea.

Chapter 7

As soon as she stepped off the parking lot curb onto the grass, Eleanor and her harp case were engulfed by a throng of costumed musicians who shouted their glad greetings and swept her off to a white tent.

"Come back around noon," she called before she disappeared. "I've got free lunch tickets!"

And there we were, standing on the edge of the burgeoning revelry. A group of caftan-clad flower children glided by us leaving the lingering aroma of burning hemp in their wake. Children and dogs frolicked on the lawn, and I could hear bongo drums in the distance.

It was the moment I'd been dreaming about for weeks. Despite the crowd, I was alone with Olivia, and a whole unfettered day stretched ahead of us. A feeling of terror mixed with exhilaration swept through me, a sensation I can still conjure just by closing my eyes and thinking back. No moment is more keenly intense than the one in which desire meets manifestation.

What was strange was that I had kissed Olivia already, at least two dozen times. I'd sung to her, held her in my arms, professed my undying love. How could it be that our lips had touched, and yet this moment of no contact—a moment in which all I was doing was standing next to her in a public place—was so thrillingly intimate?

It felt like that brief juncture of space and time when a conductor raises his baton in front of a ready orchestra. No sound exists within that instant, but somehow it contains all the music that ever was and ever will be. Olivia turned to look at me. As our eyes met, we both felt the bond form between us. Years later, we talked about it, how it was like the string on Ben Franklin's kite, just before the lightning struck.

"Thanks for inviting me," I said when I couldn't stand the tension any longer.

"Thanks for inviting me to the Gala," Olivia replied. She looked at me, then quickly looked away. "I'm sorry I—"

"It's okay," I said quickly. "You don't have to apologize."

"No," Olivia said firmly. "I really am sorry. I kept wishing you'd ask me again, so I could say yes. But I knew you wouldn't, so—"

"You actually want to go?" I asked incredulously.

Olivia looked at me again, and I noticed that her cheeks were a little pinker.

"When you asked me, I thought it was a trick." She paused and took a breath before continuing. "I thought you were one of them."

I gazed at her in astonishment. How could she have thought such a thing when I had tried so hard to defend her? But the answer was simple. She didn't know.

"I would never hurt you." I said.

We fell silent again, our eyes still locked. Again the tension mounted.

"So do you want to go to the Gala?" I asked, realizing after the words escaped that I could have phrased my question a little more politely.

"I guess so, if you do," Olivia said, "but actually, I don't really like that kind of thing. Too fake. Too much hairspray."

"I don't like formal dances, either," I said. "I just wanted to be with you."

As Olivia looked at me, I thought I saw doubt in her eyes. If I did, it quickly vanished, and she smiled.

"So here you are," she said. "Stuck with me for a whole day. What do you want to do first?"

Hold you and kiss you for real, I wanted to yell, but instead I said, "I don't know. I've never been to one of these things before."

"Well, then, let's start with the limberjack man. He's my favorite."

I thought she said "lumberjack" and wondered what Paul Bunyan would be doing at a music festival as she led me through the crowd. We passed a puppet show, and a man in a harlequin costume playing a marimba.

As the happy music washed over me, I kept thinking how ridiculously sheltered my life had been. I knew all about expensive restaurants and sitting in the Founders Circle at the Dorothy Chandler Pavilion. Polo games, yacht races, celebrity golf tournaments—all old hat. But until my trip to New York with Mr. Van Doren, I had never experienced a big city on foot or ridden on a public bus. Until today, I suddenly realized, I had never mingled with the masses. The closest I'd come was summer camp, and my mother had been as selective as possible in that department, too. God, Bill was right all those times he'd called me Little Lord Fauntleroy. As I tagged after Olivia, it dawned on me that she might not want a prince from Mulholland Drive. I watched her greet a juggler and hug a woman in a fringed leather dress holding a Native American drum, and I couldn't help worrying that I might not be good enough for her.

Now, as I look at this fabulous violin, it's all so clear. Olivia didn't need a fake Lancelot to rescue her. I needed her to save *me*.

"There he is," Olivia said, pointing toward a small stage. A boy about my age was playing a banjo, and a man with a craggy face and bushy white hair was sitting on a stool. A flat slat of wood was sticking out to one side from under him, and a long stick rested on his thigh. Attached to the end of the stick was a jointed wooden doll, and as the man moved the stick, it clattered its legs in time to the music like a little Irish dancer. The limberjack!

A crowd of children was pressed up against the edge of the stage, completely enthralled. We drew closer, and I found the performance entrancing, too. When the banjo player finished "Oh! Susanna," I applauded with the rest of the crowd. As the boy bowed and jumped off the stage, Olivia looked at me and laughed.

"You've never seen a limberjack before, have you?"

"Never."

"Come on."

As we moved closer to the stage through the scattering children, the white-haired man caught sight of Olivia.

"Livie!" he shouted.

"Uncle Chase!" she called back.

The man hopped down off the stage and wrapped Olivia in a bear hug. Then he pulled back. He was about my height, but much thinner. He was wearing a vest with lots of pockets, faded jeans, and Mexican sandals.

"Who's your friend?" he asked.

"This is Ted," Olivia said. "He's a violin player."

Uncle Chase eyed me.

"A fiddler, eh?" he said.

"A violinist," I corrected, and the instant I did, I regretted it. Uncle Chase's eyes narrowed under his bushy eyebrows, and a sly grin spread across his face.

"Well, excuse me," Uncle Chase said. "A violinist. Is he any good, Livie?"

"He's very good," Olivia said seriously. "He's going to the Juilliard School next year."

I stared at Olivia, horrified. I hadn't told her about Juilliard, but obviously, word had spread.

"Well," I began, blushing again, "actually, I still don't know for sure—"

But Uncle Chase had already disappeared into a little tent behind the stage.

"He owns a folk music store in Goleta," Olivia said. "He's a friend of my mom's. I've known him since I was nine."

Just then Uncle Chase popped back out of the tent with a violin in each hand.

"Try this on for size," he said, and before I could stretch out a hand, he tossed one toward me.

I caught it by the neck, and stared at Uncle Chase. What kind of nut throws a violin?

"Tune up," he commanded, handing me a bow. Still shocked, I turned to Olivia for help. I had no intention of playing a strange instrument even if it belonged to someone she called "Uncle."

But Olivia was smiling at me, and I couldn't bear the thought of wiping that look off her face. I turned to Uncle Chase again. He was tuning the other violin. Damn. There was no way out.

My next surprise was that the "fiddle" Uncle Chase had thrown at me looked like a decent violin, and the bow seemed perfectly serviceable, too. I had no idea what was going to happen next, but it was a huge relief to know that the instrument I was holding wasn't something cobbled together out of a cigar box and a yardstick.

As soon as we finished tuning, Uncle Chase hopped back up on the stage. Very slowly, he played a sweet, simple tune. Later, Olivia told me it was a folk song called "Star of the County Down," but I had never heard it before. An audience began to gather as he played, but when he finished, no one clapped. Why not? I wondered, but when all eyes turned on me, I suddenly knew. It was my turn.

Once again, I looked at Olivia, hoping against hope she'd get me out of this. But she was still smiling so happily that there was nothing I could do but climb up on that silly little stage. I raised my bow and played the tune Uncle Chase had just finished. When I was done, the small crowd in front of the stage clapped. I blushed, embarrassed that I was getting applause for a piece a five-year-old could have played. I was about to step off the stage when Uncle Chase launched into another tune.

This one I recognized. It was "Simple Gifts," a hymn I'd learned at summer camp when I first began to play. Uncle Chase embellished it a little, and he winked at me as he played. The moment he finished, he pointed his bow at me, and once again, the audience, all eyes on me, remained silent. With a jolt, I understood. This was no mere performance. This was a duel.

I was relieved to realize that Uncle Chase was challenging me. I wasn't ready for a practical joke, but competition was something I understood well. I stepped forward, raised my bow, and played "Simple Gifts" slightly faster than Uncle Chase had, and with a few more flourishes. I didn't quite have the nerve to point my bow at him when I was done, but I did bow my head slightly to the audience's enthusiastic applause.

I was still looking down when the first strains of Prokofiev's Sonata for Two Violins fell on my ears. I yanked my head up and gaped at Uncle Chase. This guy was no "fiddler," at least not by my snobby schoolboy definition. He was playing a piece only a virtuoso could handle. Thank God Mr. Van Doren had insisted I master it just a few months before. By the time it was my turn to play, I had collected myself well enough to enter right on time.

I couldn't believe what was happening. Here I was, playing a strange violin outdoors on a rickety riser with a guy in huaraches for a bunch of people wearing headbands and paisley bedspreads. What is even more incredible is that we actually sounded good. The crowd around the little stage grew. When we finished, the applause was long and loud. Piercing whistles rose above it, along with shouts of "Encore!"

Uncle Chase took a bow, but I just stood there, hoping desperately that if he launched into another duet, it would be one I knew. He was trying to humble me, after all, and now I had no doubt he could do it.

Uncle Chase straightened up and beckoned me to the center of the stage. Taking his cue, I bowed with him to another prolonged round of applause.

When I raised my head, I was alone.

Uncle Chase had jumped off the stage. He was standing next to the banjo player, smiling expectantly. The audience seemed enormous now, a sea of faces, all waiting. But for what? I hadn't signed up for this! My first impulse was to hurl my violin at Uncle Chase, grab Olivia, and flee.

Then I looked at her. She was right in front of me, and sunlight outlined her body through the white gauze of her dress. A breeze, ever so slight, caught the ribbons on the wreath of flowers in her hair. My eyes met hers, and I can still remember her face. She wasn't smiling. She was gazing at me, studying me. Suddenly I knew that it wasn't Uncle Chase's opinion that mattered, or anyone else's in that endless audience. My eyes still on hers, I raised my bow.

I launched into Paganini's "Last Caprice in A Minor," the same piece I'd chosen for my audition. But there the similarity to my Juilliard performance ended. In New York, my cocky confidence, carefully honed over nine years of top-notch mentoring, was enough to carry me through with perfect precision. There, in front of an audience of professional critics, I'd had no doubt I was "good enough." But here, on an uneven platform in a public park in California, I had no such self-assurance.

For the first time in my life, I was worried about my audience. Until now, I had always thought Mr. Van Doren's advice about "staying in the music" really meant "ignore all ears that happen to be lurking nearby." An audience was just a necessary evil, and the secret to a good performance lay in pretending it didn't exist. Even in New York, when I imagined Olivia was listening, I was still playing in solitude.

But now she was six feet away from me in the flesh, terrifyingly present, and no amount of denial could banish her from my awareness.

A few bars into my piece, I admitted that Olivia was inside my private universe, and tagging right along behind her were Uncle Chase, the banjo player, and four million hippies. My carefully constructed fortress had been thoroughly breached. How could I possibly "stay in the music" with a horde of barbarians inside my gates? God only knows how I kept on playing.

And then it happened. The solitary citadel I had taken such pains to build and defend exploded in an eruption so exhilarating I felt like I'd swallowed fireworks. Suddenly I realized that music doesn't need the protection of a moat, and neither did I. The idea was as silly as trying to trap sunlight in a closed box.

Until that day, I'd always thought of music as an unruly horse. My job was to break it, harness it, and ride it with the unflinching discipline of a master of dressage. If it weren't for that unexpected performance in Isla Vista Park, I would still be taking tightly controlled steps on a safe and well-worn path. If it weren't for Olivia, I would never have realized that a lifetime of taut reins and clenched thighs is nothing compared to one second bareback on an unbridled Pegasus.

I finished my piece, and for an oddly long moment, the audience was silent. A dog barked, and I could hear the marimba in the distance. Then, like a rogue wave, the applause rolled in, gaining in volume and intensity until I was engulfed. Uncle Chase leapt back up on the stage and held my arm up as though I had just won a boxing match, and a woman rushed forward with a flower wreath. She placed it on my head and straightened the ribbons down my back. Through it all, the applause continued. At last, Uncle Chase led me off the stage, and the audience began to disperse.

After he took the violin from me, Uncle Chase shook my hand and put his arm around Olivia.

"You're right, Liv," he said. "He's not bad." He lowered his unruly eyebrows and squinted at me. "Almost good enough to call himself a fiddler."

The day was completely different after that. Everywhere we went, people smiled. I had Olivia at my side and flowers in my hair. Isla Vista Park had metamorphosed into a paradise beyond all imagining.

In the afternoon, after we'd had lunch with Eleanor, we sat on a lawn near a man playing a hammered dulcimer.

"New York," Olivia said suddenly.

"What?"

"Isn't that where Juilliard is?"

"Yes."

"It's a long way away."

"Farther than you think," I said. "My father won't let me go, even if I get in."

Olivia looked at me. "Why not?"

"He's a stupid jerk."

Olivia was silent for a moment, then spoke so softly I had to strain to hear. "At least you have him," she said.

Oh, God, I thought. How could I have said something so thoughtless?

"I'm sorry," I managed to stammer. "I didn't mean to—"

"It's okay. I never knew him. He died before I was born."

Olivia's hand moved to the gold chain around her neck, and she pulled a little heart-shaped locket from the bodice of her dress. Snapping it open, she held it close, so I could see the two little photographs that faced each other inside. On the left was a smiling, dark-eyed man wearing a Santa Claus hat. On the right was a little girl with her hair in pigtails. Olivia.

"He died a week after Christmas," she said. "This was the last picture my mom took of him. He was playing Santa for my cousins."

What do you say to a girl whose father died? I stared at her, utterly without words.

"It was an accident," Olivia said. She paused, and I struggled to think of something—anything—to say.

"He died instantly," she continued. "Or anyway, that's the story."

I must have murmured something along the lines of "I'm so sorry" because Olivia patted my hand.

"It's okay. It was a long time ago."

A long time ago. How the meaning of that phrase shifts and changes as we grow older. Olivia's father had died only fifteen years before. It's been more than twice that long since I sat next to her on the grass in Isla Vista Park, but it's as vivid as yesterday.

"My dad was originally from Mexico," Olivia said. "He and my mom met in high school, when he was a senior, and she was a sophomore."

She glanced at me as a tinge of pink colored her cheeks. "Just like us," her look said, and my heart swelled. Just like us.

Except not really, I learned, as Olivia told me the rest of the story. Eleanor and Javier both dropped out of school to get married. Javier worked two jobs, one delivering newspapers and another cleaning swimming pools. On a rainy New Year's morning, a Cadillac ran a red light on Olympic Boulevard and collided with his motorbike. Three months later, Olivia was born.

When Olivia was nine, she and Eleanor moved from Los Angeles to Santa Barbara to live with Eleanor's mother's sister. Aunt Emily taught English at a public high school, and she helped Eleanor get a job as a teacher's aide. Eleanor also worked as a bartender on weekends.

"That's how she met Rick," Olivia said. "Her old boyfriend. The first time I met him was at my tenth birthday party. He brought me a Barbie, and I thought he was nice. I was even happy when he and my mom got engaged—at first, anyway."

Olivia stopped talking and gazed at me intently. I could see thoughts swimming behind her eyes, as though she were debating whether to tell me more. Not knowing what else to do, I stayed silent, and at last Olivia spoke again.

"Rick was a monster." She paused again, her face serious. "He never hit me, but one night when Aunt Emily wasn't home, he broke my mom's wrist. And she still has a scar where she cut her forehead falling against the dining room table.

"My mom managed to make him leave, but he came back on his

Harley after she got back from the emergency room. He drove it right up the steps onto Aunt Emily's front porch. He broke all the potted plants and smashed the stained glass window in the front door. The police had to come and take him away in handcuffs."

Olivia looked at me, then reached up and straightened my wreath.

"You look good with flowers in your hair," she said before going on with her story. "Aunt Emily said it would be a waste of time to try to get the police to protect us from Rick. He was only in jail overnight, and she said we should vanish before he could get drunk again.

"We left town in my mom's station wagon, because it was still pretty new and we were afraid Rick would wreck it if we left it behind. We drove to Mr. Steiner's house—you know Mr. Steiner?"

"The old guy who coaches the debate team?" I asked.

"Yeah. He used to teach at Aunt Emily's school in Santa Barbara. He moved to Ojai when he retired."

When he heard about Eleanor's predicament, Mr. Steiner suggested that she apply for the position of live-in housekeeper at Haviland.

"My mom didn't really want to be a cleaning lady, but we needed a new place to live, and she liked the idea that I could go to Haviland for high school if she worked there. She wants me to go to college."

Olivia paused and looked at me. "She says my dad wouldn't have died if they hadn't gotten married so young. If he'd finished high school, he never would have been out delivering newspapers in the dark. But who knows?" She shook her head as if to rid herself of the thought, then reached down and plucked a dandelion from the grass in front of her. She twirled it in her fingers, then turned to look me square in the eyes.

"You were really great today, Ted."

"What?"

"On the violin. You were perfect."

Even now, all these years later, I can almost hear her saying the words, almost catch the scent of her hair. "You were perfect."

But she had it all wrong. I wasn't perfect, as my story will too soon reveal. Perfection belongs instead to Olivia and her gift to me that day. Although I couldn't have known it then, she gave me my violin career. I might well have gone on to become an adequate musician, but Olivia deserves credit for everything I ever achieved beyond that.

We wandered the festival until the sun began to set. Before we went back to school, Eleanor took us to dinner at Carmen's, a tiny Mexican restaurant with brick floors, whitewashed adobe walls, and a resident parrot that said, "I like your chiquita, man," whenever you so much as looked at it.

When we got back to Haviland, I stood with Olivia at her front door while Eleanor parked the station wagon.

"Were you home when Rick drove his motorcycle onto your aunt's porch?" I asked. I hadn't been able to get the image of a freaked-out Hell's Angel out of my head since she told me about him.

"Yeah, I was," Olivia said, her eyes widening at the memory. "I'll never forget it. It was something like three in the morning, but I hadn't been asleep all that long because we spent so much time at the emergency room. This huge crash woke me up. Then there was an even huger crash, and breaking glass. I rushed out onto the balcony over the front door, but it was freezing, so I ran back inside and grabbed this old purple knit afghan off my bed. I wrapped myself up, went back outside, and watched."

She paused, then smiled. "It was like a movie. The whole neighborhood was out on the street, and three police cars. I was so happy when they took Rick away. I hated him for what he did to my mom."

I didn't kiss Olivia that night. I shook her hand. I thanked her mother and headed across campus to my dorm.

Lying on my bed, I relived the whole day, from our ride through the orange groves to the parrot at Carmen's. In my dreams, I was Lancelot again, but everything was mixed up. My steed was no longer a horse. I was a crazy nutcase on a Harley-Davidson motorcycle, and Guenevere smiled down upon me from a balcony, wrapped in a purple afghan.

Chapter 8

Three days later, Olivia and I were in the light booth in Goddard Hall, a few minutes before rehearsal was supposed to begin. Bill Cross had just stepped out to find a screwdriver, and his two freshmen hadn't arrived yet.

"I've never been in here before," Olivia said, scanning the collection of ramshackle furniture and assorted junk Bill had managed to cram into the small space. "It's like a secret clubhouse or something."

She plopped down on a beanbag chair stuffed into one corner. "I like this," she said. "And hey, it's big enough for two."

Even as dense as I was, I recognized an invitation when I heard one. I tripped on an extension cord as I rushed to join her and fell against her as I sat down. We were face to face. Her cheeks were flushed, and I sucked in a breath.

"Olivia—"

And I kissed her. It was only a peck, really, and sort of lopsided. But God! It was real!

"Teddy."

She touched my cheek, and I stared into her eyes. *Teddy!* No one ever called me that except my mother, and I made her stop when I was seven. "It sounds like a stupid stuffed toy," I'd explained.

But now, damn! I wanted nothing more than to be Teddy. I was about to kiss Olivia again when we both heard voices outside the door.

I leapt to my feet, crashing into an orange crate and knocking over a lava lamp. When Bill opened the door, I had just saved it from smashing on the linoleum.

"What the hell are you doing, Spencer?" he yelled as Russell and Katsu, the two freshmen, peeked curiously around him. "I'm going to have to suspend your light booth privileges if you aren't careful." He looked from me to Olivia and back. "You should both know that this room has only two functions. Lights—"

He flipped on the overhead and moved to a turntable. Lowering the arm onto a record, he twisted the volume knob.

Baby, baby, that thing you give to me …

Bill held out his arms. "And love." He stretched the word out into three syllables, and the two freshmen giggled.

"Thanks, Bill," I said, and I meant it. "And thanks for sharing. I'll work at being less of a klutz."

Haviland had rules against public displays of affection, and the teachers did their best to keep interactions between boys and girls as platonic as possible. But even the strictest rules were no match for Olivia and me. She sneaked brownies into the library at night, and we ate them in my favorite nook. I memorized her schedule and met her in the short breaks between classes. Best of all were the minutes we stole before play rehearsals in the light booth. Bill instructed Russell and Katsu to keep watch in the hallway when he wasn't around to do it himself. All of them became very proficient at coughing loudly whenever Mr. Harper's footsteps approached.

No doubt Mr. Harper knew what was going on. As rehearsals went on, I noticed that he found more and more reasons to be in the light booth before we got started. His suspicions, however, probably greatly exceeded anything that actually happened in Bill's lair. Mostly Olivia and I just sat on the beanbag chair, held hands, and talked.

When we did, it seemed we were no longer sitting in the light booth in Goddard Hall. We were no longer schoolchildren. All names and labels fell away, and we traveled the cosmos together.

I know we spoke about our lives and our futures, but what lingers with me most from those ecstatic hours is the fundamental connection we shared. On the surface, Olivia and I were as different in background as any two students at Haviland could be. But on a deeper level, we were the same. We spoke the same language, dreamed the same dreams. We shared a current in some ethereal stream. We bared our souls and swam together there. We were one. We were free.

When I think back on it now, over decades of experience, a cold desolation sweeps over me, and tears jump to my eyes. I know now that the connection I shared with Olivia was as rare as moon rocks. I know now that I should have done everything in my power to hold her close, to never let her go. How did I not know it then, when I was wrapped in that indescribable joy? How did I let her slip away from me? Why did I fail to do everything in my power to pursue her? I have no answer. Despairing, my heart beats the familiar refrain that has murmured there all these years: *If only. If only. If only.*

On the second of April, I was in the mailroom, which was really just an alcove off the dining hall with pigeonholes lining one wall. The room was crowded, as it always was when word spread that mail was "up."

Without warning, Amanda Woodmancy let out a piercing shriek.

"Oh, my God!" she shouted, pulling an envelope from her box. "Stanford! And it's fat! Oh, my God!"

She ripped open the envelope and emitted another shriek.

"Yes! Yes! Yes!"

Amanda leapt up and whacked the wrought iron chandelier hanging above us, sending it swinging dangerously near the ceiling. Usually only guys did that, but Amanda was a basketball player and a bit of a tomboy.

I pulled my mail out of my box, and a letter similar to Amanda's slipped onto the floor. She was quick to scoop it up.

"Oh, my God, Spencer! You got a fat one, too—from Yale!"

I grabbed it from her, and she held out her hand. There was nothing I could do but paste on a smile and shake it.

"Congratulations, Amanda," I said, and, stuffing my letter into my jacket unopened, I pushed through the crowd back into the dining hall. I had ten minutes before my chemistry lab, but I decided to head on over to the science building anyway. If I was lucky, I'd catch sight of Olivia on the way, at least from a distance. Her PE class was supposed to be playing field hockey today.

The path to the science building ran behind the top row of bleachers, and a group of sophomore girls had gathered on the field below, "suited up" in their pleated blue tunics. But where was Olivia? I paused, wrapping my arms around myself.

I felt the fat envelope inside my jacket, the envelope I had dreaded. I hadn't even opened it. It only heralded the unavoidable truth: The end of the school year would separate us. Olivia was only in tenth grade. She'd spend two more years at Haviland. No matter what, I would be banished to somewhere else. Even a fat letter from Juilliard was beginning to seem like unwelcome news. New York, as Olivia had pointed out at the music festival, was a long way away.

Where was she, anyway? I wondered. The girls had started their game, but Olivia wasn't among them. Sighing, I trudged on to my chemistry class. Olivia, I learned later, had gone to Santa Barbara with her mother. Aunt Emily was in the hospital with pneumonia.

Chapter 9

Easter vacation began on Friday, and my mother drove up to Haviland in her Mercedes convertible to collect me. The first thing she said after she kissed me and ruffled my hair was, "Your father and I are so thrilled about Yale." I must have replied civilly, because I didn't start a fight. My mother chattered happily all the way to Los Angeles, detailing my schedule for the coming week, the coming months, and the rest of my life. I just watched the ocean go by and tuned her out as best I could.

I wished Olivia could have come home with me. Hoping it might be possible, I didn't invite Bill Cross as I had done every other year. He loved spending vacations with me because my parents were nicer to him than his own were.

"They'd be happy if I just disappeared," he used to say about his mother and father. "Maybe one of these days I just will."

I know Bill was disappointed, but he didn't let on.

"Mr. Gillespie wants me to stay with him," he said, "and I think it'll be fun. His hobby is rockets and blowing stuff up, and his wife makes chocolate chip cookies by the gross."

I felt terrible that my best friend was suffering the ignominy of spending a vacation on campus with the science teacher, and I felt even worse when it turned out that Olivia couldn't come home with me after all. Even though Aunt Emily was home from the hospital, Eleanor made it clear that both of them would be spending the week in Santa Barbara to look after her while she recuperated. But maybe it was just as well. All week long, my parents kept making plans for my future, and I was glad Olivia wasn't around to hear them.

The only break I got was when the Halls came over for dinner. They were longtime friends, and their daughter was almost exactly my age. Both families had home movies of Karen and me playing naked in a backyard wading pool, and it was a standing joke that they'd be screened at our wedding reception.

Karen was pixie-like, with straight, white-blonde hair. When she was younger, she rode horses and took ballet lessons. Now a senior at a girls' school in Holmby Hills, she'd switched from tutus and jodhpurs to Carnaby Street fashions and British rock music. Tonight she was wearing an orange knit top and a lime green miniskirt. It wasn't a style I warmed to, but she did have the body for it.

"Why don't you take Karen to a movie?" my father suggested when it was time for the grownups to have their coffee and cognac. Karen liked the idea, probably for the same reason I did: It was an easy escape.

After weathering a serious barrage of nudges and winks, we pulled out of the driveway in my mother's Mercedes. That was a privilege. Usually, I was only allowed to drive a vehicle my father called "The Beater." "The Beater" was actually a meticulously maintained Jeep station wagon my father took on fishing trips, but I was still happy to get the chance to cruise Sunset Boulevard in a red convertible. The only thing keeping it from being a perfect evening was that Karen would be riding shotgun instead of Olivia.

"What do you want to see?" I asked, realizing a little late that we should have checked the newspaper before leaving.

"We don't have to go to a movie, Ted," she said, batting her extended eyelashes at me. "I just got a good new fake ID—"

"No."

"Dork."

Karen sulked as we headed down the hill, but she perked up by time we got to Hollywood. I found a place to park near the Cinerama Dome, and somehow we managed to arrive at the box office just in time for the 9:40 screening of *The Graduate*.

"Have you seen it?" I asked.

"Like it matters," Karen said. She blew a huge pink bubble and let it pop on her nose. I couldn't remember a time when she didn't have gum in her mouth. At least I won't have to buy her popcorn, I thought as we crossed the lobby.

Karen cracked her gum the whole time, but even that couldn't distract me from the movie. I'd had no idea what *The Graduate* was about, but from the moment Dustin Hoffman appeared on the screen, I was spellbound. Benjamin Braddock was just like me, I thought, and Elaine was Olivia. The only thing that didn't fit was Mrs. Robinson because I couldn't imagine having two love affairs at once, and I would never in a million years have an affair with my girlfriend's mother. Take out Mrs. Robinson, though, and the story was mine.

It's only now, all these years later, that I understand why the movie had such an effect on me. I would have screamed denial, but I actually *was* pursuing two love affairs at once. The only difference between me and *The Graduate* was that my Mrs. Robinson was a violin.

"I hated it," Karen said as we walked back to the car. "If I found out my boyfriend was sleeping with my mother—oh, frick, it's just too gross!"

I opened the passenger door for her. "Let me drive," she said.

"No."

"Come on. You can't possibly be that much of a dip."

"You don't have a license."

"I have a learner's permit."

I don't know why I gave in, maybe just to avoid further confrontation, but I handed Karen the keys. She surprised me by driving very carefully, almost too slowly. When we got to a dark stretch of Mulholland Drive, she pulled over in a spot that had a view of the city.

"Why're we stopping?"

"I dunno. Look at the view." Karen rummaged through her purse and pulled out a Kleenex. Extracting the large pink wad from her mouth, she wrapped it up and dumped it back into her bag. We sat, looking at the lights. It was a clear night, and they sparkled.

"I'm kinda cold." Karen shifted closer to me, and I looked at her in astonishment. She was doing everything a boy is supposed to do. What next?

"Don't you want to kiss me?" she asked.

Not wanting to say no, I stayed silent.

"We all know what this means, Ted," Karen said. I turned to stare at her. "I've been suspecting it for a while now."

"What?"

"You're a fag."

I burst out laughing, and Karen was so surprised she started laughing, too.

"Who is she?" she asked after we'd fallen quiet again.

I didn't answer, and Karen curled up a fist and thumped my thigh.

"Well, whoever she is, I sure hope she likes violin music."

"Where are you going to college?" I asked, deliberately changing the subject.

"Smith or Wellesley, whoever says yes first."

"Still the all-girl thing," I said. "Maybe *you're* the fag."

The Halls left shortly after Karen and I got back to the house, and my parents went upstairs. Wishing I could talk to Olivia, I paced the downstairs hall and ended up in my father's study. A large room paneled in mahogany, it smelled like stale tobacco. I sat down in the leather swivel chair behind the huge desk and turned on the lamp.

In front of me was a black tray. It was divided into little white satin-lined compartments. In almost every one, a gemstone sparkled in the lamplight. My father had recently taken up stone faceting as a hobby. He'd converted half of the wine cellar into a workshop, but this was the first time I'd seen any of the results. I picked up what looked like an amethyst and turned it in the light. There were several translucent blue stones, too, and a red one I figured must be a ruby.

Then I saw the diamond. It was the size of a small marble, and it sparkled with the slightest tinge of pink when I held it up to the light.

"Nice piece of ice, don't you think?"

I looked up to see my father in his bathrobe. He moved to the desk, picked up a lighter, and held it to his cigarette.

"It's yours, son," he said. "For when the right girl comes along."

Hastily, I dropped the diamond back into its little padded compartment. My father chuckled.

"No rush, Ted, but I mean it. I had you in mind when I cut that one. It'll be here waiting for you."

Easter vacation was far too long. For most kids, it's a week, but boarding schools usually add on a couple of "travel days" to accommodate students who live far away. Every day I fantasized about sneaking back to Haviland in "The Beater." As tempting as the idea was, I didn't act on it. The dorms were officially closed, and students weren't allowed on campus unless they had special permission, like Bill Cross. Instead, I called Olivia every day when my parents weren't paying attention to me. I knew all the long-distance calls would show up on their phone bill, but by then I'd be back at school and beyond caring.

April was half over when I returned to Haviland. My mother drove me again because my father had left on a business trip to Chicago the day before. Once again, she chattered all the way, but this time I found myself participating. Her plans for my life were infinitely easier to take when I knew I'd see Olivia in two hours, one hour, fifteen minutes, ... *now.*

She was standing in the road next to the dining hall when we drove up. She was wearing her faded jeans and V-neck sweater, the same outfit she'd had on when she invited me to the music festival. When she saw me, she waved both hands above her head.

"Who's that girl?" my mother asked, and I spoke the name that had dominated my thoughts and dreams for the past ten days.

"Olivia," I said, and then I yelled it at the top of my lungs. "Olivia!"

Chapter 10

Remember how Dustin Hoffman screams at Katharine Ross at the end of *The Graduate* so she won't marry the wrong guy? That's how I yelled at Olivia. I howled as though my life depended on her reply. And maybe it did. Maybe it does now. Should I step outside right this very moment and shout her name into the wind?

But unlike Dustin Hoffman, I'm too late this time. Olivia is a continent away, and only the Merino Rose remains to prove she was here at all.

"It's for you, Teddy," she said when she left it here. "You're the one who can make it sing."

Am I? It's true I've played magnificent violins on stages from Sydney to San Francisco, but what's a perfect concert worth if I myself was mute when life called for a crescendo? I look again at the Merino Rose and resist a fleeting impulse to smash it to matchwood.

"Olivia." I say her name aloud, and it summons Yo Yo, my noble Siamese. He leaps up on my lap. Another leap and he's on my keyboard, typing gibberish with his paws and purring a loud request for an ear rub.

"Olivia." I whisper her name again as I pet my cat. Am I really the same guy who bellowed at the very sight of her?

My mother was shocked at my outburst, and even more so when I leapt out of the car without opening the door. It was a chilly day, but so beautifully clear that we'd driven up the coast with the top down anyway. I raced to meet Olivia and wrapped her in a hug.

By the time I turned back to call her, my mother was out of the car herself and walking toward us carrying my suitcase.

"This is my friend Olivia de la Vega, Mom," I said, still slightly out of breath.

"Olivia, this is my mother, Ann Spencer."

"I'm so happy to meet you, Olivia," said my mother, looking at me instead of her. "Ted's told us so much about you." It was a lie. I'd said nothing. I stared back at my mother as Olivia smiled and murmured a polite reply.

My mother left shortly afterward, saying that she supposed the next time I'd see her would be when she and my father would drive up to see *Camelot* the second Saturday in May.

"We'll stay at the Hunt Club," she said. "Maybe you can join us for brunch there on Sunday." She seemed to be including Olivia in the suggestion, and she waved cheerily as she drove away down the hill.

"Your mom is nice," said Olivia as we watched the car disappear around the first bend. "I'm glad I got to meet her." I didn't say anything. I just turned and looked at her. A sudden breeze whipped her hair away from her face. She shivered slightly. I took her face in my hands and kissed her.

"I missed you, Olivia," I said.

"I love you, Teddy," she replied.

I love you.

Right out there in the open, where we were breaking all the rules, we kissed again and again and again.

I checked my mailbox after dinner. It contained only one piece of mail, a fat envelope from Juilliard. I was alone in the mailroom this time, and I ripped it open. But as I scanned the letter I'd been hoping to receive, I was racked with conflicting feelings. Part of me wanted to hit the chandelier like Amanda Woodmancy did when she got into Stanford. Another part wanted to scream like Prometheus when the eagle was tearing out his liver. I'd gotten what I'd asked for, and yet it seemed to be propelling me inexorably toward all that I dreaded most. A confrontation with my parents was guaranteed, and I'd be leaving Olivia no matter what.

Classes resumed, but I could barely concentrate as I fretted about how I was going to inform my family about my intention to break the Yale tradition. The troubling scenario replayed itself again and again in my imagination, and I wondered if I could actually face my father without crumbling. Could I really avoid saying something like, "Dad, would it be all right with you if—?" I had always sought permission, never announced any plans of my own. I practiced and practiced, but when the real moment came, I seriously doubted I would be able to declare with unwavering conviction, "I've decided to accept Juilliard's offer of admission."

And of course there was Olivia, whose very presence intoxicated me and intensified all my fears at the same time. On Tuesday night, when her mother thought she was in bed, and I, too, was presumed to be under my covers in the dorm, we met at a spot near her mother's cottage. Olivia had suggested we rendezvous there.

"I used to bring my dolls here when I was younger," she said. "I called it my secret garden." It was really just a patch of grass next to the maintenance building, but the fence around the garbage dumpsters, a hedge, and two plump juniper trees created a fairly private enclosure, and there were no invading lights anywhere nearby.

"Just tell them," said Olivia after I had confided my concerns about my impending confrontation. She kissed my cheek and gently brushed an unruly curl back from my forehead. "It's your life, not theirs."

"But it's not only about school, Olivia," I replied. "It's about you—us.

Without a word, Olivia kissed me on the lips and then rested her head on my chest. I took her hand, entwining my fingers in hers. We sat there in the darkness long enough for the moon to disappear.

"You know I'll be back," I said at last, squeezing Olivia's hand more tightly. "You know we'll be together as soon as we possibly can, and nothing will ever separate us again."

Olivia didn't reply, and I thought I felt her shoulders shake ever so slightly. But when she raised her face to mine, her eyes were dry.

"I know you'll be back," she said quietly. "Teddy, we were meant to be together." I looked into her eyes as a single tear, caught in the starlight, stole down her cheek.

I kissed it away, and then my lips found hers. If I allow myself, I can still remember the taste of her tears, the scent of her hair, the promise of her touch. How long we held each other, I don't know, but the memory is as indelible as the sound of the Merino Rose. Olivia and I could separate for a century, but like the haunting music of a fabled violin, she would never leave my heart.

"We will be together forever as soon as we can," I said at last, stroking her hair. "In the meantime, we'll write every day, and I'll call, too. And I'll be home for holidays and vacations—every chance I get." Olivia remained silent as my mind filled with plans and hopes for the future.

"I've got to tell my parents soon," I said suddenly. "I've got to get it over with." Until that moment, I'd been assuming I'd tell them when they drove up to see *Camelot*, but why wait?

Three days later, Eleanor de la Vega's station wagon rattled down the Haviland hill with me at the wheel. Olivia was at my side, and the car was headed south to Los Angeles.

Meanwhile, at a mansion on Mulholland Drive, Edward Spencer III was selecting wine to serve to his dinner guests while his wife Ann went over the final details of the menu with the cook. Allan and Lynette Hall were expected at seven, along with Donald and Davida McLaren. Not one of them had any idea that Lancelot and Guenevere would be arriving at eight.

Chapter 11

Olivia had suggested borrowing her mother's car, and Eleanor de la Vega approved of the plan, as long as we promised to drive directly to my parents' house and return by dinnertime on Saturday.

"No detours," she insisted. "I don't care how inviting the beach looks. You don't even need to stop for gas. The tank's full." She handed me the keys to the station wagon and added, "Keep it under the limit, Ted."

We left campus around six and headed south past Lake Casitas, emerging at the edge of the continent just before sunset. I glanced at Olivia as the fire of the descending sun reflected on the ocean and turned the old Chevy into a golden coach. I can still remember her profile bathed in that spectacular light, her green eyes reflecting the brilliance.

And then she began to sing.

I joined in, and we sang all the songs from *Camelot* as we rolled inland through Oxnard, Thousand Oaks, Calabasas. All my fears were forgotten in the bliss of singing those familiar songs with Olivia. A physical memory of that pure, unfettered happiness occasionally ripples through me when I lose myself on the violin, but never since have I shared that feeling with another person. Oh, Olivia. How I wish we had kept on driving that night, rolling on to the horizon and another day, another day together.

But we didn't, of course. We were good kids. I got off the freeway at Beverly Glen and dutifully headed up to Mulholland. It wasn't until I rounded the bend and saw my family's house ablaze with lights that all my fears came crashing back down on me.

Why so many lights? I wondered, and then I saw the cars. A Cadillac and a BMW were parked along the circular driveway. Damn. I hadn't imagined that my parents might have company.

We pulled up behind the BMW, which I now recognized as belonging to the Halls. Damn, I thought. Is Karen here, too? I hoped not. My mother had grilled me about our "date," but I had failed to convince her that "date" was the wrong word for our trip to see *The Graduate*.

I didn't have much time to worry about Karen, though, because I caught sight of my father through the living room window. I watched him move immediately toward the front door, and I knew exactly what he was thinking: Who in hell was parking such a crappy old wreck in the Spencer driveway?

At least Olivia and I were dressed well. I was wearing pressed khaki slacks and a tennis sweater, and Olivia had on a simple, long-sleeved dress that matched her green eyes and fell modestly to the tops of her knees. Her hair fell straight and smooth down her back, and the only jewelry she wore was her heart-shaped locket.

As my father walked toward the car with a look of puzzled annoyance on his face, I rushed around the hood to open Olivia's door. By the time she emerged, he had reached us.

"Ted!" he said, still puzzled as he looked from me to the car to Olivia. "What a surprise!"

"I know, Dad," I hurried to answer. "I'm sorry I didn't call."

Damn! I was apologizing already.

"And who might this be?" asked my father, bestowing a stiff little smile on Olivia.

"Uh, this is my friend Olivia de la Vega, Dad," I said. "Olivia, this is my father, Edward Spencer."

"I'm so pleased to meet you, sir," said Olivia without a trace of nervousness.

My father nodded at her and turned to me. "Come on inside, son," he said. "We're about to eat."

All things considered, dinner was fine. My mother, after getting over her initial surprise, seemed genuinely pleased that we'd come. She was extra nice to Olivia, and the table was quickly reset with two more places. Both the Halls and the McLarens were pleasantly friendly, and Karen wasn't there. As we sat down to a dinner of poached salmon and asparagus, I actually felt relieved that we had arrived in the midst of a party. It postponed the inevitable.

"So you're Guenevere," Mrs. McLaren said to Olivia as the maid cleared the main course. "I saw Julie Andrews as Guenevere on Broadway. It's a big role."

"Wow, you're lucky," Olivia said. "I've listened to the soundtrack a thousand times, but that's nothing like seeing her on stage. Was she wonderful?"

"She was," Mrs. McLaren said, "and Robert Goulet was a wonderful Lancelot. But I'm sure you two will be even better."

"Thanks. You're right about Ted, anyway. He's got a great voice."

I blushed as everyone winked at me, but I was relieved that Olivia seemed perfectly at ease chatting with my parents' friends. As I was continually discovering, Olivia was capable of taking care of herself wherever she landed. She had perfect manners, and she wasn't the slightest bit stiff.

"Karen's in a show this semester, too," Mrs. Hall said. "Westlake's doing *Guys and Dolls*." She looked at Olivia. "Karen's our daughter. She and Ted have been friends since they were babies."

"Where do they get the boys?" I asked, mostly to change the subject.

"Some from Harvard School, some from Beverly Hills High. Too bad you aren't closer. You could have tried out, too. Karen would have loved it."

Fortunately, my mother had decided on cherries jubilee for a grand finale, and the cook was a real showman. Just then, he dimmed the lights and set the dessert on fire. The flames took Mrs. Hall's mind off Karen, and when they died down, my father started pontificating about Barry Goldwater.

The guests left around eleven. My father refilled his snifter as soon as he had closed the door behind Dr. and Mrs. McLaren. As he sank back down onto the living room sofa, my mother came in.

"Olivia, dear," she said, "why don't you come with me? I'll show you the rest of the house and get you settled in one of the guest rooms."

The two vanished down the hall before I could say a word. All I could think was: This is it. The moment had arrived. It was time for me to declare my intentions, not only about school, but also about Olivia.

"Tell me about her, son," said my father, as though he had read my thoughts. "Who is she?"

"I told you," I replied defensively. "Olivia de la Vega. She's a sophomore at Haviland."

"Where's she from?"

"What? You mean her family? Santa Barbara."

"You know what I mean."

I knew exactly what he meant. Anger boiled within me as I recognized his prejudice against her Hispanic name, and my outrage grew as I realized I could never erase it. The only good thing about my father's comment was that it made me change the subject, and my fury gave me the strength to speak my mind without apology.

"I've decided not to go to Yale."

There was no reply from the couch, and my father took a hefty slug from his snifter.

"Juilliard accepted me. I'm going."

My father didn't say anything, which was exactly the response I'd dreaded. When Edward Spencer III took his time formulating a rejoinder, it was a sure sign it would be deadly. He was known in the business world as a venomous negotiator, the kind who coiled and bided his time before making a strike. I watched him set his snifter down and lean forward to the marble coffee table in front of him. Opening a cloisonné box, he extracted two cigarettes. Even more deliberately, he lit one using the carved alabaster table lighter next to the box. Placing it between his lips, he sat up again and drew in his breath. The end of the cigarette blazed orange, and he removed it from his mouth. He held it toward me.

"Care for a smoke, son?"

"I—I don't smoke, Dad," I stammered. He had never offered me a cigarette before, and I had never smoked in his presence.

"Oh," he said, and he was quiet again. I just stood there, watching my father take another drag on the cigarette, and at last he spoke again.

"I don't know what this is all about, Ted," he said, "but I shall assume you'll come to your senses after this play into which you've been investing so much energy is over. We'll talk again then. Good night." He paused, then continued, "I assume you've made sure that—that vehicle out there isn't leaking oil on the driveway. In the morning, please move it out onto the street."

I couldn't believe it. I'd been summarily dismissed, and nothing at all was settled. Uncontrollable rage rose inside me.

"No!" I shouted. "No! I will not move the car onto the street. It can stay right where it is, and you can damn well get used to it!" I paused, barely able to see through my anger. My father remained silent.

"And I'm going to Juilliard. And I love Olivia. We're going to get married."

The words were out there, where a thousand horses couldn't pull them back. My father took a slow sip of brandy before he answered. Then he picked up the cigarette from the edge of the ashtray on the table and held it toward me again.

"If you do that, son," he said at last, "this cigarette is the last thing you'll ever get from me."

Chapter 12

I didn't know whether my father was threatening me about Juilliard or Olivia, but I didn't stick around to ask. Shocked fury engulfed me as his words rang in my ears. My own father had actually used the old "no more money" threat, and I wasn't about to stick around and beg him to change his mind. He was an arrogant old bigot, an autocratic tyrant. *Damn him!*

I rushed into the foyer, and if there was a rational thought in my head, it was probably that I'd go to my room, which was at the top of the sweeping staircase in front of me. But something made me turn down the hallway to the back of the house instead, and a moment later, I was opening the French doors that led to the patio between the swimming pool and the tennis court. Chilly air struck my face as I stepped outside. The pool and surrounding garden were dark.

Impulsively, I stripped off my clothes and dropped them on a chair next to the patio table. The cold night air made me shiver as I walked to the diving board at the far end of the pool, but I was so hot with anger I hardly noticed. Even when I hit the water, I barely felt the shock. I swam the length of the pool and emerged dripping at the shallow end.

I grabbed a towel from the cabinet next to the tennis court fence and wrapped it around my waist. Gathering my clothes, I headed back inside. I was still furious, but the night air and the cold water had begun to cool me down. The fight with my father was far from over, and my mind was already working on a counterattack.

Just beyond the kitchen, another hall branched off from the main one at a right angle. It led to the game room, the wine cellar, and the guest rooms. I glanced down the hall. Light leaked out from under the door of Olivia's room and the bathroom next to it. She was still awake.

I paused and listened. The house was quiet. My mother, I was sure, had retired to the second floor. My father—who the hell cared? Even so, I took pains to be silent as I crept down the hall.

When I reached the bathroom, I heard the sound of water running. Olivia was taking a shower. I was clad in nothing but a towel, and Olivia was naked less than ten feet away. I should get away from here, I thought. This is wrong.

Instead, my heart beating wildly, I knocked softly on the door and stepped back. I waited, breathing hard, and the sound of water stopped. The door opened inward about two inches, just enough for Olivia's eyes to peek around the edge.

The door opened further, and Olivia, still dripping but wrapped in a large towel, drew me inside.

She was about to say something, but this wasn't a time for words. I pulled her toward me and kissed her harder than I ever had before. I clasped her body close and felt myself harden against her through the towels. Oh God, I thought. This is wrong, but I can't help it. I'm wrong, and I can't help it. I kissed her, and I was glad we were both already wet. Maybe my tears wouldn't show.

At last Olivia pulled away a little. Holding my face between her hands, she kissed my forehead, my eyes, my chin.

"It's okay, Teddy," she said. "I love you." She stepped back an inch or two more, and her towel fell to the floor. I looked down and was shocked to see that my own had already fallen. We were naked.

Transfixed, I stared at her, and I can still remember how beautiful she was in the half-light. Slowly, we moved together again, and I have never forgotten the ecstasy of her skin against mine, her arms around me, and mine around her. I kissed her neck, her face, her lips. We stood there panting as we gazed into each other's eyes. I could feel both our hearts beating.

Again the tears came, and this time I didn't care if Olivia knew.

"I love you, Olivia," I said when I found my voice. "I always have. I always will."

"I love you, too, Teddy. I really believe that we are meant to be together."

"I believe that, too," I said, but a lifetime of proper training made me pull away. "And we will be together. I promise."

I didn't sleep that night. I lay in my boyhood bed awake until the sun crept in around the shades. All night I tossed as I thought about stealing back down to Olivia's room. She was so close! Nothing prevented me from tiptoeing quietly down the stairs and creeping along the hallway. Don't even think about it, I commanded myself. The right time will come, and this is not it. Like it or not, we must wait.

But, oh God! How long? If I'd known then how long the wait would be, I swear I would have rushed downstairs and bashed her door in. I would have ripped away anything that stood in the way of consummating our connection, and I feel certain that Olivia would have wanted to do the same. *We were meant to be together.* She said that. I know she meant it, and I know she was right. But here I am, sleepless once again without Olivia, and I'd do anything, even destroy this fabulous violin, if it meant that I could hold her in my arms.

In the morning, breakfast was served on the patio between the tennis court and the pool. An observer would have seen a perfect family gathering. My father smoked and read the *Los Angeles Times*, and my mother made small talk about the weather and her roses and *Camelot*. I should have smelled a rat, but I was too busy staring at Olivia.

After breakfast, my father asked Olivia if she'd like to see the gemstones he was working on, and she readily agreed. I was left sitting at the table with my mother as Olivia followed my dad into the house.

Ann Spencer cut right to the chase. "Your father and I are tremendously disappointed about your suggestion that you might not attend Yale."

Suggestion. Might not. That wasn't what I had said, and there didn't seem to be any reason not to point out that fact.

"I've decided to go to Juilliard. I was good enough to get in, and I'm going to study violin."

My mother rearranged the roses in the vase on the table before she answered.

"Olivia seems to be a very lovely girl."

I held my tongue as anger began to boil up inside me.

"Where is her family from?"

It was too much. I leapt up from the table, jarring it enough to upset the vase of roses. My mother caught the vase in time to prevent it from breaking, but water splashed all over her sweater, and the roses scattered on the table. She shook herself off and blotted the water with a napkin, all the while maintaining a perfect calm.

"Her father was from Mexico, but what the hell difference does it make?"

"Oh, come on, Ted, I didn't mean to upset you. She's a very lovely girl. You just caught your father off guard when you said you wanted to marry her."

"I will marry her. I love her."

My mother was silent as she refilled the vase from the water pitcher and began rearranging the scattered roses.

"Ted, your father and I have decided that if you really want to attend Juilliard, we won't stand in your way. It's tremendously disappointing to us that you've decided against Yale, but we're proud that you qualified for Juilliard. If you want to go there, you have our blessing."

Had I heard right? I stared at my mother as she put the finishing touches on her flower arrangement. She said nothing more, and the happy truth began to register. I had my father's blessing, which, roughly translated, meant he'd be paying my bills. Hot damn! I was going to New York!

Chapter 13

I told Olivia how things had gone as we drove toward the coast, but I omitted the parts that betrayed my parents' prejudice. There was no reason for her to know about their bigotry, I reasoned, never imagining what they might have said to her when I was out of earshot. I should have wondered why Olivia was so quiet on our drive back to school. We didn't sing, and Olivia didn't even hum.

We arrived back at Haviland three hours earlier than we'd promised, which seemed to both please and surprise Eleanor de la Vega.

"I hope you kids had a good time," she said when I handed her the car keys, and we both murmured an affirmative response.

"Thank you so much for letting us borrow your car," I added. "It drove great, the whole way."

"It leaked oil on your parents' driveway," Olivia said quietly. "I hope you won't get into too much trouble for that."

I stared at her. Had she overheard my conversation with my father? Impossible, I told myself. Olivia must have noticed the oil spots herself.

"It's no big deal," I said, and I was right about the oil spots. It would be a very long time before I found out how wrong I was about everything else.

We plunged back into our classes and the last three weeks of *Camelot* rehearsals. Even though Olivia and I were together more than ever in the final flurry of preparation, it seemed harder and harder to find moments to be alone.

Then my mother called.

"Karen's eighteenth birthday is next week," she said, "and the Halls have organized a little dinner dance at the country club on Saturday—"

"No, Mom," I said. "I'm swamped, and—"

"Just listen a minute. I'll come get you in the afternoon, and I'll bring you back first thing Sunday morning. This is the last year you'll be able to do things like this, and Karen's your oldest—"

She didn't have to finish. "Karen's your oldest friend" was the same line she'd used to get me to go to her debutante ball.

"Okay," I sighed, "but I've got to be back by ten Sunday morning. I've got rehearsal."

I decided not to tell Olivia about my command performance. It seemed unnecessarily mean to tell her I was going to a dance with another girl. And anyway, Karen's party wasn't something I was doing for enjoyment. It was an obligation. I was only going to keep my parents happy, which in turn was supposed to make things better for Olivia and me. Only now do I see the folly of this logic. I wasn't being noble at all. Once again, I was just avoiding confrontation.

That night, I met Olivia in the secret garden. Even though it was April, the nights were still cool. Olivia had brought her old purple afghan, and we sat wrapped in it, our backs against the stucco wall and our knees bumping together.

"I have to go home for dinner on Saturday," I said. "My aunt's in town just for the weekend."

Olivia didn't say anything, and to fill the silence, I went on.

"My mother's sister. From Philadelphia."

Olivia remained silent.

"You okay?" I asked. It was dark, and I couldn't see her face.

"It's just that I miss you," she said. "You're still here, and I already miss you."

I put my arms around her and felt her warm tears on my cheek.

"Don't cry, Olivia," I said. "All we have to do is make it through the next two years."

But words couldn't dry her tears that night.

Karen's party wasn't the only thing that ate into my ever-decreasing amount of free time. Graduation was drawing closer. I was class valedictorian, which meant I had a speech to write. In addition, there were all sorts of twelfth-grade traditions I couldn't ignore, like "Ditch Day" and "Grad Night." At the end of May, the senior class always took a five-day trip to San Francisco, and the day before Commencement, we were supposed to host a big picnic for the rest of the school. And somehow, amid the crush of activities, I still had to find at least four hours a day to practice my violin.

Looking back with the clearer vision of hindsight, I see now that there was something affecting my mood beyond my impending graduation. In the wake of my parents' decision to support my choice of college, I was relieved and excited. Even though it would take me away from Olivia, I was happy with the way things were turning out, and I couldn't hide it. I was blind to the pain she must have suffered as I surfed through the last weeks of school on a tall wave of giddy anticipation. I actually believed I had succeeded in getting everything I ever wanted.

Camelot fueled my ebullience. The show was nothing less than perfect, and most of the credit went to Olivia. But it wasn't just her flawless performance that set the production above most high school efforts. Thanks to Olivia, we all tried harder and did better than we ever would have without her. By the time the curtain fell on the third and final performance, the jealousies that had launched *Camelot* were forgotten, and Mr. Harper was lauded as a genius for "discovering" Olivia.

My parents were waiting for me in Goddard Hall when I emerged from the dressing room after the show. "You were wonderful, Ted," my mother said, kissing me and fluffing my hair. "We knew we had a violinist in the family, but we had no idea we had an actor, too."

I looked around, but Olivia was nowhere to be seen. Eleanor had been sitting in the front row only a few seats away from my parents, but she was gone, too.

"Fine work, son," said my father, clapping me on the back. "You've done us proud."

I was distracted, still scanning the thinning crowd for Olivia.

"Well," said my mother, patting my shoulder, "we know you've got a cast party to go to, so we won't keep you. We'll be back to pick you up in the morning for brunch. Say ten o'clock?" I agreed without clarifying whether the plan included Olivia, and my parents moved away. Where was she, anyway? I began to search in earnest, but when I didn't find her, I gave up and headed to the post-production celebration in the dining hall.

Olivia was perched on the edge of a table, clad once again in her favorite faded jeans. Bill Cross was lounging next to her, along with Russell and Katsu. They were drinking Cokes and laughing. I stood there for a moment and watched, realizing that I couldn't remember the last time Olivia had laughed like that with me. A pang of jealousy welled up in me, but I shook it off and moved toward her.

The moment our eyes met, Olivia stopped smiling. She slipped off the table, and set down her Coke. Seeing the purpose in her face, Bill and the two freshmen hung back.

"Olivia, you were—" I began, but she laid a finger against my lips before I could say another word.

"I need to talk to you, Ted," she said. "In private. Go to the secret garden now, and I'll be there in ten minutes."

It was the usual plan, designed to keep us from getting caught breaking school rules. I lingered a few moments after Olivia blended back into the party and then made my unobtrusive escape to the enclosure next to the maintenance building. I sat down on the grass, leaned back against the stucco wall, and waited.

I hadn't been sitting there more than five minutes when I heard the soft sound of Olivia's feet on the pathway. As it always did at her approach, my heart began to beat a little faster. I rose to my feet as she slipped between the juniper tree and the hedge, and I held out my arms as she moved toward me.

"Olivia," I whispered, "I—"

"Shh," she replied. "We have to be extra quiet. I saw Mr. Gillespie on my way over here, walking his dog in this direction."

Puck deserved a walk. Defying all who feared he'd suffer a nervous breakdown on stage, he had performed admirably in the footlights.

We sat down quietly and waited for the jingle of dog tags to pass. Olivia spoke first.

"Ted," she said, and I heard the seriousness in her tone immediately. "Ted, I—"

I tried to kiss her, but she pulled away.

"I have to tell you something."

My heart stopped. It already knew this was bad.

"Ted, we can't see each other anymore."

Was I hearing right? I stared at her in the dark.

"I'm going back to the party, but I wanted to tell you in private."

I'm going back to the party? I was too stunned to say anything for a moment. Olivia started to get up, but I grabbed her arm.

"Wait!"

She sat back down and hugged her knees.

"Why? What did I do? What's wrong?"

Olivia was silent for a moment or two.

"Everything's wrong, Ted. You. Your parents. Your friends. Your violin. Everything."

What was she talking about?

"I love you, Olivia."

"Well—" She paused a moment, her chin resting on her knees. "I don't love you."

This time I didn't try to stop her when she stood up.

"I hate you," she said. "You're a liar and a cheater."

The words cut into me like a blade. What was she talking about? What had I done? A horrible silence fell between us. I stood up, but it was too dark for me to see her face.

"And you're a snob."

I still didn't know what to say, and after a couple more wrenching moments, Olivia turned on her heel, slipped between the shrubs, and disappeared.

I just stood there, unwilling to believe that my world had just been shattered. What had I done? Finally, I made my way back to my room and threw myself on my bed without taking off my clothes. If I slept that night, I don't remember it.

Chapter 14

The next morning, still in shock, I forced myself to shower in time to meet my parents. They picked me up at ten, and somehow I managed to survive brunch at the Ojai Valley Hunt Club and a drive to Santa Barbara afterwards. My mother insisted, saying that it was our last chance to do it as a family.

"Things will be too hectic after graduation, Ted," she said. "And after that, we won't have a good excuse to come here anymore."

When I got back to campus, I immediately headed for Olivia's house. It was against school rules for me to go there without an invitation from Olivia's mother, but I didn't care. I didn't care about anything except getting Olivia to talk to me. I had to find out why she was so angry. What had I done? How could I get her back? At the very least, I told myself, she owed me an explanation.

Eleanor's station wagon was parked next to the cottage, and my heart pounded as I walked up the little concrete path. Taking a breath, I rapped my knuckles on the door, then stepped back and waited. No one answered. I knocked again, but there was still no movement inside. I waited a moment and knocked a third time as I resigned myself to the fact that no one was home.

I scoured the campus, hoping to find her. I searched the library first, and then headed to the gym on the off chance she was hanging out with the Sunday afternoon volleyball crowd. I wasn't surprised that she wasn't there, and she wasn't in the rec room next to the dining hall, either. I walked back to my dorm, cursing the fact that the next morning, I'd be on a bus to San Francisco with all the other graduating seniors. The trip was supposed to be a reward, but now it would be nothing but torture until I returned on Friday.

After dinner, I made another trip to Olivia's house. Once again, no one answered the door, and I trudged back to my room. An empty suitcase lay open on my bed. Damn. The bus was leaving at six the next morning, and I had done nothing to prepare. But I won't be able to sleep, I told myself, so what difference does it make? I'll have all night to pack. I reached for my violin case, which I always kept on the shelf over my desk.

My violin. Right then, I hated it. I hated everything about my privileged life. Even though I still had no idea what I had done to make her so unhappy, Olivia was right when she called me a snob.

Sighing heavily, I pulled the case off the shelf. It was stupid to blame my violin. It was the one thing in my life that would always be there for me. Unlike Olivia, it could never decide to hate me, and right now, it offered escape. For three hours, I could put myself on automatic play, and afterward …

No, I told myself when I emerged from the practice room. It's too late. It was after ten o'clock, and school rules were clear. I had permission to be out of the dorm after hours, but only to practice. I was now supposed to go directly to my room.

But rules didn't matter anymore. I couldn't stop myself from detouring by Olivia's house. Maybe she'd be out taking a late walk, or I might even find her in the secret garden. I had to see her before I left for San Francisco. I had to! I crept stealthily along the path, trying to make as little noise as possible.

Eleanor's car was still parked where it had been earlier, but the cottage was completely dark. I stood there staring at it, my heart beating wildly. If I knocked and Eleanor answered, would she let me see Olivia? Of course not. And what if they were asleep? The last thing I wanted to do was to make Eleanor angry and give Olivia another reason to hate me.

Moving silently back down the path past the maintenance building, I slipped into the secret garden. Still breathing hard, I set my violin case on the sloping wooden slats of the cellar door next to the electric meter. Maybe I should sneak back and knock on Olivia's window. I knew which one it was, even though I'd never been in her room. I could tap softly, so she'd hear me only if she were still awake. But I'd never done it before—we'd always planned our meetings.

On sudden impulse, I reached for my violin case, flipped open the clasps, and raised the lid. My violin gleamed in the light of a naked, moth-enshrouded bulb on the corner of the building. I grasped the neck and lifted it out. I picked up my bow.

I knew if I played, the sound would carry. Olivia's window was no more than twenty yards away, and once her mother had heard us laughing from her living room. She hadn't figured out exactly where we'd been, but we were always more careful after that. Several of the teachers' cottages were also within easy earshot of the secret garden. On a quiet night like this, music might even reach the dorms.

But who the hell cared, as long as Olivia heard me? I tucked the violin under my chin, and raised my bow. Taking a breath, I played the first note of Paganini's "Last Caprice in A Minor." As the sound sliced into the silence, I was shocked at how loud it was. I'd probably wake the whole campus! But the thought only made me continue. If everyone could hear me, Olivia could, too. Exhilarated, I played on, certain that at any moment, she would slip between the juniper trees.

But as I played, and Olivia didn't appear, doubt crept into my confidence. Could she actually listen to me play this piece—the same one I had played at the folk music festival—and still not come to find me? How could the connection we shared be severed so suddenly? How could life be so unfair as to give me Olivia and then yank her away? I blinked back sudden tears and struggled to continue.

Just then, the lower branches of one of the juniper trees moved. I sucked in a breath but kept playing. They moved again as Puck, Mr. Gillespie's sheepdog, pushed his way into the secret garden. Following at the end of his leash was Mr. G. himself, armed with a flashlight. I stopped playing.

"I knew it had to be you, Spencer," Mr. Gillespie said. "What gives?"

"Nothing," I said. "I'm just—I'm going back to the dorm."

"You sound great, but it's late."

"I'm sorry," I said.

Mr. Gillespie patted my shoulder. "Get some sleep. You've got an early call tomorrow."

He watched as I packed up my violin, and he held the juniper branches aside as I stepped back out onto the pathway.

"If it's real, it will survive."

I turned to stare at my teacher.

"Trust an old guy, Spencer." He paused to untangle Puck's leash. "And get some sleep."

When I got back to my room, I sat down at my desk. Maybe Olivia was too sound asleep, I told myself, or maybe she wasn't even home. Even though her mother's car was there, it was possible that Aunt Emily had picked them up. Or maybe … it didn't matter. All

I knew was that I couldn't get on the bus in the morning without making one last attempt to communicate with her.

Opening a spiral notebook, I began to write on a blank page. After ripping out at least a dozen false starts, I carefully copied this letter onto a piece of the engraved stationery my parents had given me for my seventeenth birthday.

> *Dearest Olivia,*
>
> *I have to see you. There are things—important things—I must tell you. Please, will you meet me in the secret garden at 5 o'clock on Friday? I'll be on the senior trip to San Francisco until then.*
>
> *If I'm not there, it will be because the bus is late, and I'll get there as soon as I can. If you're not there, I'll know what it means. I won't understand, but I'll know.*
>
> *Olivia, I love you. I always have. I always will.*
>
> *Teddy*

The next morning, I put the letter in Eleanor's mailbox, where I had so often left messages for Olivia before. Then I got on the bus with the other seniors and began counting the hours until Friday afternoon at five o'clock.

Chapter 15

Everyone else on the senior trip noticed the Golden Gate Bridge and Coit Tower, but I didn't. I was too busy scouring every souvenir shop I came near for the perfect gift for Olivia.

It didn't take Bill Cross long to figure out that something was up.

"Lovers' spat?" he asked when he found me eyeing a large, heart-shaped box of chocolates at Ghirardelli Square. I didn't answer, and a couple of minutes later, he stepped in front of me holding a five-pound plank of solid milk chocolate.

"Take her this," he said. "She can't help but be impressed."

"I don't want to impress her," I said. "I just want to talk to her."

"She'll laugh at you if you take her that stupid heart, Ted," Bill said. "That's what you give a floozy." I didn't agree, but on the off chance he was right, I settled on a two-pound assortment wrapped in silver paper, tied with satin ribbon, and topped off with a red silk rose.

Before the bus headed back down the coast, I also found one other gift, a tiny gold replica of the Golden Gate Bridge set with a single small diamond. I showed it to Bill on the trip home. When he saw it, he shook his head.

"Diamonds are dangerous, Spencer," he said. "Women can't help thinking they mean marriage."

I didn't say anything. I just closed the little box and slipped it back into my pocket. Gazing out the window, I spent the whole journey hoping Bill was right.

The bus arrived on campus a little after four o'clock on Friday afternoon, but I couldn't wait until five to see Olivia. I dropped my suitcase off in my room, slipped the little jewelry box into my jacket pocket, slung the Ghirardelli shopping bag over my shoulder, and set off at a dead run for her house. I forced myself to slow down as I turned the corner past the science building, hoping to catch my breath before I knocked on the door. As I headed down the last stretch, I noticed a black pickup truck parked next to Eleanor's station wagon. I was still wondering what it meant as I reached the juniper trees next to the maintenance building.

Just then, I heard a laugh. I froze. It was Olivia! She was already in the secret garden! She must have arrived early! My heart leapt, but just then, another laugh broke the silence. A deep laugh. A male laugh.

For a long, shocked moment, I stood there paralyzed. Then, clasping the shopping bag against my body to prevent it from rustling, I leaned forward until I could peer between the branches.

Olivia was sitting cross-legged, her back against the stucco wall of the maintenance building. Next to her—their shoulders nearly touching—sat a guy in jeans and cowboy boots, his long legs stretched out in front of him. He was at least twenty, maybe even older. He had black hair and stubble on his chin. I'd never seen him before. As I stood there in disbelief, he reached over and patted Olivia's knee. She smiled, and he said something in what sounded like Spanish.

Olivia's hand moved to the gold chain she always wore around her neck. Pulling out the heart-shaped locket and snapping it open, she held it out to her companion. He moved closer and took it in his hand. He gazed at it, then at Olivia. Then, leaning closer, he kissed her cheek.

My heart stopped. I stared at Olivia's face as he pulled away. She was smiling, and she patted his knee.

Shocked tears sprang to my eyes as I turned and ran. I didn't stop running until I was back in my room. Panting and sobbing, I flung open my wardrobe and stuffed the shopping bag into the bottom, back behind my shoes. I slammed the door and threw myself onto my bed. Then, leaping up again, I pulled the little jewelry box out of my pocket and threw it across the room. It ricocheted off the door, hit the floor near my desk, and disappeared behind my wastebasket.

Chapter 16

That was it. Olivia had made herself clear. The bond we had shared was broken, and all that was left for me was the rest of my life. On graduation day, I gave my mother the Ghirardelli chocolates and the gold charm. She loved them, and my father congratulated me on my thoughtfulness.

I've often wondered what might have happened if Olivia and I had not parted. To fill the vacuum she left in my life, I threw myself into my music, and I did well enough at Juilliard to earn even my father's grudging respect. I was a student there when I won the Whitworth Award and played my first concert as a soloist at Carnegie Hall, and I landed a position as assistant concertmaster with the Vienna Philharmonic as soon as I graduated. At twenty-one, I was the youngest violinist in the orchestra, and the only American.

As high school disappeared into the past, I made no attempt to keep in touch with anyone I had known there. I even lost touch with Bill Cross. He'd gone to USC after we graduated from Haviland, but that was all I knew until the summer of 1977. I was visiting my parents, something I did every August during the Vienna Phil's summer hiatus.

"Bill Cross called last week," my mother said soon after I arrived. "It was so good to hear from him after all this time. He's a lawyer now. He left his number."

My old buddy was a lawyer? I smiled at the thought, but it didn't really surprise me. Anyone with Bill's talent for talking himself out of scrapes would make a first-rate attorney.

"Let's have lunch," Bill said when I called. "Come by my office, and we can go from here."

Bill's office was in a Century City high-rise. I parked in the subterranean garage and took an elevator to the top floor. A pretty receptionist greeted me from behind a marble counter. Bill, dapper in a dark pin-striped suit, emerged through an etched glass door.

"Ted!" He shook my hand and slapped my shoulder. "It's been too long! Come on!" I followed him to his office. It wasn't large, but its glass-and-stainless-steel furnishings were very chic. It also had a spectacular view to the west.

"Damn, Cross," I said. "You've come a long way from the light booth in Goddard Hall."

He sat down behind his huge shiny desk. He looked small.

"I guess I have," he said, "but—" he sighed and ran a hand through his hair.

"What?"

"Oh, I don't know. It's just not what I thought, I guess. Hey, did you know I got married?" He turned a framed photograph around. A cute sunburned brunette in shorts and a bikini top was standing on a beach. "Last October," he said. "Lisa's expecting a baby in December."

"Wow," I said. "Congratulations."

Bill laughed. "You sound surprised, but you're not half as shocked as I am. It's like I've suddenly become everything I never dreamed of. A tax lawyer, a homeowner, a husband—and God—I just bought a stroller the other day." He shook his head and plucked a thread off his sleeve. "What about you?"

I shrugged. "Just the violin."

"Hey, that reminds me," Bill said, sliding a file drawer open. "I've got something for you." He pulled out a newspaper clipping and held it out to me.

"What is it?" I asked, but my question was unnecessary. I stared into Olivia's face smiling from the entertainment section of the *Los Angeles Times*. Bill waited while I read the accompanying story about the burgeoning success of a local television show called *Meatloaf*. It was a cooking program featuring Jay Conklin, a stand-up comic who was also a chef. According to the article, the real appeal of the show was not Jay but the "Chopper Chick," his lovely assistant. A large photograph showed the "Chopper Chick" smiling as she diced onions. "Olivia de la Vega raises a knife along with the ratings for Conklin's *Meatloaf*," read the caption.

"That's why I called your mom," Bill said. "I wanted to get your address so I could send it to you." He pulled out another clipping and slid it across the desk toward me. "Here's another one," he said, "from just a few days ago. Looks like *Meatloaf* was her big break."

I scanned the story, a short piece from *Daily Variety*. Olivia would be joining the cast of *Gunther*, a CBS detective drama.

"You didn't ever get back together with her, did you?" Bill asked.

"No."

"Idiot."

After a leisurely lunch at a French restaurant in Pacific Palisades, I drove Bill back to his office.

"Come to Vienna," I said before I left.

"Yeah, it's on my list," Bill said. "In between twenty-hour days and changing diapers."

"Well, anyway, let's keep in touch."

But we didn't.

Chapter 17

After my afternoon with Bill, I caught sight of Olivia's likeness more often in newspapers and magazines, even in Europe. *Gunther* turned out to be a good career move, and soon Olivia was being cast in films. She got what she wanted, I marveled to myself: a successful acting career. Somehow, given her background, her achievements seemed far more impressive than my own. I found myself proud to mention, when her name came up in conversation, that I had known her.

"We went to high school together," I would say. "We were both in *Camelot*. She was Guenevere. I was Lancelot." That always got a reaction.

"You've kissed Olivia de la Vega?" people would cry. "You lucky dog!"

I'd smile coyly, but I never said anything more. It was all just a memory, just acting, just pretend. Even though I had once believed it was something far more rare, I convinced myself that my connection with Olivia was worth nothing more than a good laugh at a cocktail party.

In 1979, the *International Herald Tribune* reported that Olivia married Jay Conklin, "her former manager." A year later, I read about the birth of their first child, a daughter named Theodora.

In early September 1985, I accepted a dinner invitation from Maria Gürtler and her husband. Maria was a cellist who had taken me under her wing when I first came to Vienna. She and Dieter helped me find my first apartment.

"Come over Monday night," she said. "We've invited a few friends for a pig roast." She winked and patted my cheek. "Including someone I'm eager for you to meet."

Maria was always trying to set me up. "You need a partner, Edward," she was fond of saying. "Do you want to grow old alone?"

When I arrived at the Gürtlers' house in the suburb of Neustift am Walde, it was obvious that "a few friends" was an understatement. Cars lined both sides of the street, and the sound of merriment was audible from the pathway to the front door. I rang the bell. It was a beautiful, balmy evening, and I turned to watch the sunset while I waited.

"Come in!"

I spun around to find myself face to face with one of the most arrestingly beautiful women I had ever seen. Her sleek black hair was drawn up in a twist, and her dark eyes sparkled as she dazzled me with a smile so warm I almost began to sweat.

Although I had only seen her from a distance, I recognized her. I was staring at Valeria Cosimano, a soprano who had just arrived from Rome to spend a season with the Vienna State Opera. She held out her right hand.

"Valeria."

"I know," I said taking her hand. "I'm Edward."

"I know." She smiled again. "Maria told me you were coming."

Heat spread through my body as she drew me into the entryway and tucked her arm through mine.

"Everyone is on the terrace," she said. "Come on."

"I need to do something with these flowers," I said. I was holding a bouquet of yellow chrysanthemums.

"Oh, of course," Valeria said. "Let's see if we can find a vase."

"Your English is perfect," I said, following her into the kitchen.

"I spent a year in Iowa when I was sixteen," she said. "Not very many people there spoke Italian." She looked at me, and once again our eyes locked. Again I felt warmth spread through my body.

We must have found a vase for the flowers, and I'm sure I spoke with Maria and Dieter that evening. I must have met their other friends, too, and I have no doubt the pig was delicious. But all I remember is Valeria.

We had dinner together the next night, too, at a tiny bistro near my apartment. The third night, I cooked spaghetti at home while Valeria made a salad. She sang as she worked, in between sips of red wine.

"You are a terrible cook, Edward," Valeria said later as we piled the dishes in the sink. "I haven't had worse pasta since Ames, Iowa."

"I guess it's more of a corn-on-the-cob kind of place," I said.

Valeria shuddered.

"American food is so horrifying," she said. "My host family served something called 'chicken in a basket' the first night I was there." Her face contorted at the memory. "I couldn't believe they ate chicken with their hands! And they seemed so shocked when I asked for a knife and fork!"

She turned toward me. Grabbing the lapels of my jacket, she pulled me close. "You're barbarians, all of you!" she said and, as if to prevent me from denying it, she kissed me. It was a fierce, hungry kiss, and it seemed to last an eternity.

"And you call *me* a barbarian?" I asked when, breathless, we finally parted.

"Well," she said with a laugh, "my mother always told me she bought me from some Magyar gypsies. Maybe she wasn't joking."

We kissed again, and now we were lucky we both had a few days without commitments. Except to eat and practice, we didn't get out of bed for the next three days.

"You owe me," Maria said when Valeria moved in with me two weeks later. She was ecstatic that one of her matchmaking attempts seemed to be such a success.

My mother was thrilled, too, when she and my father came to visit in October.

"It's as though someone turned the lights on in here," she said as she walked through my flat, "or built a fire."

She was right. With little effort, Valeria had transformed my stark bachelor's pad into a warm and elegant home. And there was no denying the heat between us.

"She's really something," my father said with a wink one night when Valeria was out of earshot. He took a final drag on his cigarette and stubbed it out. "She reminds me of your high school friend."

"What?"

"Your high school friend. The Mexican girl."

"She's nothing like her." I was surprised at the anger in my voice. I watched as my father lit another cigarette.

"Would you like a brandy?" I asked. He nodded as he clicked his lighter shut.

My hands shook as I lifted two snifters down from the cabinet over the countertop and pulled the stopper from a bottle of Rémy Martin. After I filled both snifters with hefty slugs of cognac, I picked one up and knocked it back. By the time I returned to the living room, I could feel the alcohol beginning to numb me. I handed a snifter to my father and sat down.

"I've read about her," he said. "She's done well."

I stayed silent.

"Have you stayed in touch?"

"No. She's married. She has a kid. Do we have to talk about her?"

"Not if it upsets you, Ted."

"It doesn't upset me," I said, my voice too loud. "It's just stupid."

That night, I dreamed I was searching for Olivia, but I could never quite catch up with her. "She was just here," people said wherever I went. "She's gone now."

Before my parents left two days later, my mother invited Valeria and me to come to California for a visit.

"We will, Mom," I said. "Sometime soon."

At first, I thought we would.

"I'm going to leave the Vienna Phil," I told Valeria. "I've always wanted a solo career, and then I can live wherever you choose."

"Roma," Valeria said. "I can travel the world, but Roma will always be home."

I can live in Rome, I thought. Rome is wonderful. I've always wanted to learn Italian.

But spring rolled around, and I had done nothing to begin a new career or separate myself from the Vienna Philharmonic.

"Next year, Valeria," I said. "I promise. I just need a little more time."

"I know, *tesoro mio*," she said, patting my cheek. "And in the meantime, we have Alitalia."

Valeria left in May for a summer engagement in Verona. My apartment felt the chill, even though she came to visit twice during the summer. In October, I flew to Rome.

Valeria wasn't at the airport, though she had promised to pick me up. I called her apartment several times, but all I got was a busy signal. After an hour or so, I took a taxi to her apartment building near the Theater of Marcellus. It was a relief to hear her voice through the intercom, and after she buzzed me in, I rode the elevator up to the eighth floor.

Valeria was standing in front of me when the elevator door slid open. She was wearing a silk kimono, even though it was nearly noon. Was she sick? I wondered. But she didn't look sick. She looked as stunningly gorgeous as ever. She led me down the hall to her apartment. I set my bag and my violin case on her sofa, and I took her in my arms.

"Oh, Edward! I'm so sorry!" she said, her hands curled into fists on my chest.

"It's okay. I took a taxi. I tried to call you, though. Is your phone working right?"

"Oh, Edward," she said again. "Everything is so—so complicated."

"Complicated?" I said, pulling away. If there was one thing our relationship had never been, it was complicated.

"I'm so glad to see you!" she said, pulling me back. She kissed my forehead, both cheeks, my lips. "I miss you so much every day."

She let me go. I took off my jacket.

"You are so beautiful," she said.

"What?"

"You're beautiful. I love you. You're perfect."

I stared at her.

"Oh, Edward!" Valeria burst into tears.

God! What was this? Valeria could be something of a drama queen, but I'd never seen her like this before. I put my arms around her and patted the back of her head as she sobbed against my shoulder.

"Oh, Edward, oh, Edward, oh, Edward. I'm so sorry, so sorry."

When her shoulders finally stopped heaving, I took her face in my hands and looked into her eyes.

"Whatever it is, we'll deal with it," I said.

She nodded, still hiccupping, and pulled away.

"I—just a minute," she said, and she disappeared into another room. As she did, I couldn't help noticing something. A pair of tall black leather boots stood next to the archway she had just passed through. They couldn't be Valeria's. They were huge and masculine and slightly scuffed. I was still staring at them when Valeria reappeared, dabbing her eyes with a handkerchief.

Not many women look beautiful when they've been bawling their eyes out, but Valeria was one of the few. She crossed the room, took my hand, and led me to the dining table. On it was a crystal vase holding a dozen red roses with a card nestled in them.

"Edward." Valeria pulled her chair up until our knees touched. She took both of my hands and turned her eyes up to meet mine. They filled with tears again, but her voice was steady this time.

"I'm a bad person. Evil."

I had no idea what to say, so I just stared at Valeria in silence.

"I've been unfaithful to you."

The boots. The flowers. The tears.

"Do you want me to leave?" I asked.

"No! I love you! And I promise it's over!"

But he left his boots?

"Who is he?"

"A tenor," she said, the tears spilling over. "Oh, Edward. I was so lonely."

A big tenor, I thought, looking at the boots again. A goddamn giant.

Suddenly, I had to get out of there. The boots were too big, the flowers too fresh. Moving back to the sofa, I threw on my jacket, picked up my violin, and reached for my suitcase.

"Edward, wait!"

I turned. Valeria was holding the black boots, one in each hand. She shot me a fiery look as she marched across the room and flung the front door open.

Curious, I followed her. She flounced across the hall and yanked the handle on the garbage chute. Holding one boot high, she dumped it in. I could hear it rattle and bang all the way down to street level. After the second boot made an equally noisy descent, she slammed the chute shut and blew past me back into the apartment.

Valeria wasn't finished. She strode across the room and seized the roses with both hands. She was just pulling them out of the vase when I reached her.

"Don't," I said, laying my hand on hers. "It's okay."

Valeria relaxed her hold on the roses.

"It's okay?" she said without looking at me. "That's what you think?"

"I mean they're just flowers. You don't have to destroy them."

Valeria turned a ferocious gaze on me.

"That's what you think?" she asked. "They're just flowers?"

Once again, I had no idea what to say.

"They're roses," she said. "Red roses. Do you have any idea—?"

I grabbed her and tried to kiss her, but she pulled away.

"Red roses mean love," I said.

Valeria kept her back to me.

"Does he love you?" I demanded. "Do you love him?"

Valeria whipped around, her eyes full of angry tears. "This is your fault, Edward," she said. "All your fault." She fell against my chest, weeping inconsolably like a child. I stroked her hair, and tears began to fill my eyes, too.

"I'm sorry, Valeria," I said. "I'm so sorry. I never should have let you go."

Once again, we spent as much of the next three days as possible in bed. The roses were thoroughly wilted by the time I left, and Valeria threw them down the garbage chute as we departed for the airport.

"*Finito!*" she shouted after them, and we laughed at the echo.

Chapter 18

I had every intention of keeping my pledge to leave the Vienna Philharmonic and move to Rome as soon as the season ended. I drafted my letter of resignation the day after I returned home. Now all I had to do was deliver it. What could be easier?

But somehow it wasn't easy. Although I had managed to write the letter, I couldn't bring myself to fold it up and insert it into an envelope. The letter was still lying on my desk when my phone rang a few days later.

"Hi, Ted. It's Karen."

Karen Hall! I hadn't seen her in years but she sounded exactly like she did in high school.

"I'm in Munich. It's not that far from Vienna. If I come, wanna have dinner?"

Why not? I thought to myself. Might even be fun.

"Sure," I said. "When?"

"How about tomorrow?"

She rang my doorbell the next evening.

I buzzed her in and opened my door as I waited for her to climb the stairs.

"Damn you, Ted!" she cried from the landing halfway up. "You haven't changed!"

I couldn't say the same for her. Karen was wearing a floppy straw hat and a garment that looked like a cross between a toga and a sari. Even more surprising was the backpack she slung off her shoulder and leaned against a wall.

"I've been doing the Eurail thing," she said, taking off her hat and shaking out her hair. It was longer now, and bright red. "Youth hostels, the whole bit. It was time for me to get real."

She threw her arms around my neck and planted a kiss on my cheek.

"Hungry?" I asked, and she pulled away laughing.

"Same old Ted," she said. "Maybe I should get you drunk."

But Karen was the one who got slightly hammered. I took her to a restaurant in Grinzing known for serving good local wine. I nursed one glass because I had to drive home, but I stopped counting after the waiter filled Karen's glass for the third time.

"You knew I got married, right?" Karen asked.

"Yes," I said slowly. "But I thought it didn't work out."

"Ha!" she said. "That's the understatement of the century."

I'd heard the whole story from my mother, who had tried her best to get me to attend the wedding. It took place a year or so after Karen graduated from Smith, but I was already living in Europe. I'd sent my regrets along with a crystal decanter.

Karen's parents had thrown her a wedding worthy of a queen. Her fiancé was an English guy who was a student at Harvard Business School when Karen met him. He charmed everyone with his accent and his Cambridge degree.

"He's darling," I remember my mother saying on the phone. "You should hear him quote Shakespeare. He's just adorable."

Blair didn't seem quite as adorable after the honeymoon, when he informed Karen that he had another girlfriend in London, and if she wanted to keep him, she'd have to share. Karen didn't take the announcement quietly. She and her parents hired a private detective who found out that Blair's "girlfriend" was actually another wife. He had two children and more debt than a small government.

"The bastard," Karen said. "And I thought I knew him." She took another slug of wine. "But what about you, Ted?" she asked. "I know you haven't taken the marriage plunge, but don't you have a girlfriend?"

I looked at Karen. She'd probably heard about Valeria through the parent grapevine. There wasn't any reason I shouldn't give her a few details, but I just didn't feel like it.

"She moved to Italy," I said, hoping it would be enough.

"I met someone special after Blair," Karen said. "My English lit professor at Smith. I went back for an alumnae thing seven years ago, and we really hit it off."

She paused and took another sip of wine.

"We were soul mates, genuine soul mates."

She looked at me, and unshed tears glistened in her eyes.

"Have you ever had a soul mate, Ted?"

"No," I said a little too quickly. "I mean—of course not, Karen. You know stuff like that is just an illusion. It's just infatuation. It's just hormones, for Christ's sake!"

She looked at me for a long moment.

"You protest way too much, Ted," she said at last. "And you're wrong. Finding your soul mate is the most important thing in the whole world. It's a connection like no other, a connection that unites you not only with the other person but with everything—the whole universe. I'll never stop believing that. Never." She paused to dab her eyes with her napkin.

"He dumped me," she finally continued. "Six months ago, and he didn't even have the decency to do it in person. He sent me a letter from Rome." She paused. "*Nothing of him that doth fade, but doth suffer a sea-change, into something rich and strange.*"

"What?"

"It's from *The Tempest*, but it's also the inscription on Shelley's grave in the Protestant Cemetery in Rome. Michael actually used Shakespeare to dump me, the son of a bitch."

"You were together for seven years?" I asked.

"Yeah, as much as we could be. He was married. Still is. The bastard." She drained her glass. "I wish to God I didn't still love him."

I invited Karen to stay at my place overnight, but she declined.

"I made a reservation at the Sacher," she said.

"The Sacher? That's not exactly a youth hostel," I laughed.

"Oh, I know. I stayed at the Hassler when I was in Rome, too. Don't tell anyone I'm a fake, okay?"

"You're no fake, Karen," I said. "You're about as real as they come."

"You're no fake, either, Ted," Karen said. "And I bet someday you will find a soul mate, and then you'll know what I'm talking about. It's too bad—" she paused, and our eyes met. "It's too bad we could never be the couple our parents joked about."

"They were joking?" I said.

"You're right," Karen said. "They weren't. But it's still too bad."

Later that night, after I had transported Karen and her backpack to the Sacher, I stood at my desk. My letter of resignation was still there, still waiting for my signature. On a sudden impulse, I picked up the phone and dialed Valeria's number in Rome, even though it was well after midnight.

"*Pronto,*" a sleepy male voice answered on the third ring.

I hung up. I picked up the letter and tore it to shreds.

Chapter 19

At first I was troubled by Valeria's exit from my life, but soon I began to notice that my music benefited from our breakup. Our stormy relationship had exacted a heavy price, but now all that energy could go directly into my violin. Though I kept my position with the Vienna Philharmonic, I sought and accepted invitations to perform elsewhere. It wasn't exactly the solo career I had dreamed of, but it was a big step in the right direction.

At the end of May 1987, I was in New York for a solo performance at Carnegie Hall. I had just arrived in the United States to spend the summer season at Tanglewood as a soloist with the Boston Symphony Orchestra. I planned to stay in New York for a few days before heading to Massachusetts, but my only formal commitment was my concert.

The afternoon before my performance, I retreated to my dressing room. My rehearsal had just ended, and I decided to take a walk to relax a little, something I often did during the hours leading up to a concert. I was pulling on a jacket when there was a rap on the door. I opened it to find a young Filipino holding a vase of red roses.

The flowers surprised me, but there was no mistake. "Edward Spencer" read the cream-colored envelope nestled among them. The delivery boy waited patiently while I searched for my wallet. The smallest bill I had was a twenty, and he departed with a genuine smile on his face.

As soon as he left, I tore open the envelope, wondering who had been so kind as to send me flowers. My mother, perhaps? But it wasn't my birthday. As soon as I unfolded the note, I no longer begrudged the delivery boy his generous tip.

"Dear Ted," it read in strangely familiar handwriting. "I'm in New York for a movie shoot, and I read about your concert in the *Times*. I'll be there tonight. Break a leg, or whatever it is you say to wish musicians the best of luck. Yours, Olivia."

Olivia! We hadn't seen each other in nineteen years, and now she had sent me a dozen red roses. An unexpected mixture of emotions coursed through me, mingling with a powerful surge of curiosity. She had vanished from my life so long ago, and I had always assumed I would never see her again except in films and magazines. Why had she sought me out?

Olivia's note was written on stationery from the Plaza Hotel. Was it a hint? I wondered. Did she expect me to call her? As I thought about it, I was surprised to notice my heart rate speed up. Unexpected thoughts erupted in my head, memories from an ancient volcano I thought was dead.

Calm down! I commanded myself. You're thirty-six years old, which makes Olivia thirty-four. And she's married, don't forget, with a kid. She's just an old friend from prep school. I sat down. My pulse may have slowed a little, but the tide of thoughts kept pouring forth.

Olivia had contacted me after all these years!

Convincing myself that calling to express my thanks was the only civilized action to take, I picked up the telephone on my dressing table and dialed, first information, and then the Plaza. Yes, Olivia de la Vega was registered, the hotel desk clerk informed me, but no, she wasn't in. Yes, I could leave a message.

It was nearly five o'clock. Would Olivia return to her hotel before coming to Carnegie Hall for a concert that started at eight? I had no way of knowing, but I left a message anyway, grateful that the clerk was willing to take down my words verbatim.

"Dear Olivia," I dictated. "The roses were such a surprise! Please come backstage after the concert tonight so I can thank you in person. Ted."

A wave of nervous regret rolled over me as soon as I hung up the phone. If Olivia didn't show up in my dressing room, I'd never know whether it was because she hadn't gotten my message or because she'd decided to ignore it. No sooner had that thought passed than another one arrived to take its place: You're such an idiot, Ted. You're not in high school anymore, and Olivia is only being polite. You're nothing more than old friends who happen to have washed up in Manhattan at the same time. That's all. That's it. Shut up.

I stepped outside into a cool spring breeze. Zipping up my leather jacket, I walked two blocks north to Central Park. It should have been relaxing to join the afternoon joggers and dog-walkers, but I couldn't keep my mind off Olivia. So immersed was I in thoughts of her that I stepped in front of a bus on Fifty-Ninth Street. The bus driver slammed on his brakes and leaned on his horn, and a muscular young man standing on the curb behind me seized me by the arm and yanked me back onto the sidewalk. I mumbled my embarrassed thanks and headed immediately back to Carnegie Hall, rubbing my shoulder. I was obviously in no condition to be alone on the streets of New York.

Every seat was filled for the concert, and when I walked onto the stage, all I could think about was that Olivia was sitting somewhere in the darkness beyond the footlights. For a moment, I was transported back to a small outdoor platform in Santa Barbara, to that day long ago when I had wanted to run away. I almost felt that way again as I lifted my bow. A rush of anxiety swept over me, but just as swiftly, an ecstatic thrill replaced it. I was playing for Olivia, and my wonder increased as I realized that I had never stopped playing for her. She had departed from my life, but she had never left my heart. She had vanished, but not without bestowing a priceless gift. Olivia had given me my music, and as four Mozart violin concertos filled the hall that night, I wanted her to know it.

I had planned to play Bach's Partita no. 3 as an encore, but when I raised my bow, I knew my fingers—or was it my heart?—would never allow it. I'm sure the conductor and concertmaster were startled when they heard the first strains of Paganini's "Last Caprice in A Minor." I was a little surprised myself. I hadn't played the piece publicly in years. I had consigned it to a mental vault of memories too melancholy to open, along with Olivia herself.

But not tonight! *This is for you, Olivia,* my violin sang out. *It always has been. It always will be.*

The last note was still hanging in the air when the audience leapt to its feet as one. As the waves of applause rolled over me, I gazed out over the sea of anonymous faces. Among them was the face I had never forgotten. Olivia was out there somewhere!

My nerves returned when the applause died down. Would Olivia actually come to see me backstage? The usual group awaited me in the greenroom: some friends, a few music buffs. I pasted on a smile and began shaking hands. I kept an eye out for Olivia—what if I didn't recognize her?—all the while hoping that somehow I'd be lucky enough to meet her in private, away from prying eyes and pushy fans.

The post-concert flurry didn't last very long, mostly because I didn't encourage any lengthy conversations or give anyone an opportunity to invite me out. It was extremely helpful that everyone expects soloists to be self-centered eccentrics and, on this occasion, I was happy to hide behind the stereotype. It meant that I was alone in my dressing room no more than twenty minutes after my last bow. After stowing my violin in its case, I sat down on the bench in front of my dressing table. Once again, I studied the note Olivia had sent with the roses. She still dotted the "I's" in her name with little circles, I noticed with a smile. It was such a sweetly innocent touch.

Five minutes passed, and I was beginning to think about changing my clothes. I couldn't just sit there forever, after all, and the concert had been over for nearly half an hour. Carnegie Hall is not a large auditorium. If she had really planned to come, surely Olivia would be here by now. I slipped off my black Ferragamos and tucked them in my suitcase. I had just stood up to retrieve my street clothes from the rack by the door when I heard a soft tap.

My heart stopped, and I sucked in a breath. "Come in," I managed to say.

It was not Olivia. It was another delivery boy, and he had a message for someone else. With more than a little annoyance, I sent him on his way, shut the door and removed my bow tie. Five minutes later, I was clad once again in my standard offstage uniform: gray slacks and navy cashmere pullover. I had just finished zipping my tuxedo into a garment bag when there was another knock on the door. I was standing only a couple of feet away, and I opened it.

She was wearing a simple blue silk dress and carrying a black coat over one arm. She also had on dark glasses and a scarf, which she began to remove as soon as I'd closed the door behind her. When I turned again to face her, I couldn't believe I had actually worried that I might not recognize her. Her hair, slightly mussed from being captured in the scarf, still tumbled long and dark and full, and her skin had the same wonderful golden luster. And those green eyes. The girl I had loved was still there, but there was so much more, and it went far deeper than mere photogenic beauty. Her presence filled the room when she was still standing in the doorway. "Olivia," I said, before I even knew my mouth was open. She smiled.

"Hi, Ted," she said softly as she tucked the sunglasses and scarf into her shoulder bag. "I'm sorry it took me so long to get here. I had to make a phone call. I hope I haven't kept you."

"Of—of course not," I stammered. "And—thank you for the roses. They were such a surprise. A good surprise." Olivia looked me right in the eyes.

"Were they, Ted?" she asked quietly. "I couldn't be sure." She looked down. "For me, the surprise was to get the message you left at my hotel."

"I'm glad you got it—that you're here," I said quickly. "Have you had dinner? We could—"

"Ted, I'm sorry—" My face must have taken on a look of obvious disappointment, because Olivia touched my sleeve. "No! I didn't mean about dinner. I mean, I'm sorry for, for—" She paused and took a breath. I just stood there mute, and at last she looked at me again. "Teddy," she said, and my heart leapt at the nickname, "as a matter of fact, I'm starving."

Chapter 20

For the next hour, everything seemed weird in its ordinariness. Here I was, alone with Olivia after a hiatus of nearly two decades, and the first main topic of conversation was my luggage. I had to get my suitcase and garment bag back to my hotel, and Olivia had her own mundane concerns. She was eager to avoid being recognized, and she swathed herself in her scarf again before we stepped outside.

"I hope I can get away without the sunglasses now that it's dark," she said. "What do you think, Ted? Would you know me if I passed you on the street?"

I looked at her. Even after nineteen years, even disguised with a scarf, I would have recognized her. How could that be? I wondered. I thought I had banished her from my thoughts so thoroughly, and yet—she must have been there anyway, somewhere beneath the surface.

"I don't think your fans will have a clue," I said. None of them knew her like I did, after all, and my own experience told me how easy it is to walk about unrecognized in public places. I wasn't a magazine-cover celebrity like Olivia, but I was beginning to have a coterie from my recordings and solo concerts.

"I hope not," said Olivia. "I would really like to keep the evening all to ourselves." She echoed my feelings perfectly.

We didn't have to put her disguise to the test as we left Carnegie Hall. The artists' entrance is designed to shield performers from aggressive onlookers, and we vanished into a cab without incident. Olivia had a limousine at her disposal, and I could have called a car service, but we would attract less attention in a more plebeian vehicle.

We went first to the Warwick Hotel, where I was staying. I left my bag and suitcase with the doorman, and slid back onto the seat next to Olivia and my violin. I never leave my instrument in hotels, not even in a safe. When I travel, my violin stays with me.

This particular violin was new, at least to me. It was actually three hundred years old, a wonderful Amati I'd discovered in Austria just a few months before. I could have bought a nice house in a fine neighborhood for what it cost, but it wasn't the price tag that made it valuable to me. Over the years, a good violin had become as necessary to my existence as my heart. I felt as though I'd need life support without one, and even that would ultimately fail. I truly believed I'd die without my strings.

The case was between us on the seat, and my left hand was resting on it. I was sorely tempted to move it, to remove the barrier between Olivia and me. I didn't, of course. I was afraid it might seem too forward of me.

"I have all your recordings," said Olivia, putting her hand next to mine on the case. "But they're nothing like hearing you play in person."

She had all my records?

"Thank you," I managed to say. "I've been following your career, too. Ever since I first saw a picture of you as the 'Chopper Chick.' I still watch *Gunther* reruns whenever I'm in the States, and I just got the video of *Blue Diamonds*. You were terrific."

We were silent again, but the space between us was warmer, closer. Suddenly I realized that the taxi wasn't moving.

"Oh—we better decide where we want to eat," I said. "Do you know a place, or should I go back and ask the concierge for advice?"

"I know a place," volunteered the cab driver. It is probably the only time in my life I have been lucky enough to find myself in a New York taxi with a driver who not only spoke English but was also eager to be helpful. He suggested an establishment he was sure would be open late, a restaurant in the Theater District. "You'll like Baccala," he said, winking in his rearview mirror. "Very romantic."

Olivia glanced at me with a little smile, and I felt color rise in my face. Damn! How could this be happening? She was married, and she was really little more than a stranger to me. That's what quiet reason told me, but my heart and my soul were screaming a different story.

"I've heard of Baccala," she said. "I hope we can get in without a reservation."

"Don't worry," said the cabbie. "I'll take care of everything."

He was true to his word, and his advice was well worth the large tip I gave him. Within twenty minutes, Olivia and I were installed at a quiet table in a sophisticated restaurant finished in polished granite and decorated with bronze sculptures and abstract watercolors.

"We're celebrating," I said. "Shall I order champagne?"

We ordered dinner at the same time, and while we waited for a bottle of Veuve Clicquot to arrive, I gazed at Olivia in the warm light of the candle on our table. We didn't speak for a few minutes, but the silence was far from empty. Somehow, communication was taking place without words. I couldn't take my eyes off her face. She was so familiar, yet so mysterious. I felt so comfortable, and at the same time unbearably excited.

"To Guenevere and Lancelot," I said, raising a flute when the waiter had filled them. Olivia raised her own, and we each took a sip.

"I have something else to celebrate, too, Ted," said Olivia. "You know that call I made back at Carnegie Hall? That's when I found out I'm finished shooting. I have to stay in New York for a few more days in case we need to redo a scene or shoot extra footage, but for all practical purposes, I'm done."

"To finished films, then," I said, and we drank again.

"And there's something else," said Olivia, pausing to look me square in the eyes. "When I go back to L.A., my husband and I will be announcing our formal separation. If everything goes smoothly, our divorce should be final by the end of the year."

I didn't know what to say. We just sat there staring at each other for a minute or two.

"Jay and I haven't really lived together for almost three years now," said Olivia. "We've been keeping up appearances to keep the tabloids at bay, mostly for Teddie's sake—"

"Teddy?"

"Oh!" Olivia said, blushing. "My daughter, Theodora. We call her Teddie." Olivia's cheeks were hot with color now. Damn! Had she really given her daughter my nickname? I was shocked. I was flattered. I was—damn! What was happening?

Olivia opened her shoulder bag and extracted a small photo album bound in glove leather. Opening it to the first page, she turned it toward me. There, smiling in a pink leotard and tutu, was Teddie. Her dark hair was tied into two ponytails with lavender ribbons, and she was missing her two front teeth.

"This picture's almost a year old now," Olivia said, "but that's Teddie. She says she wants to be a ballerina when she grows up."

"She's beautiful, Olivia," I said. "She looks just like you. And if she is like you, I have no doubt we'll see her name in lights one of these days."

"Did you know I never graduated from Haviland?" Olivia asked suddenly. It seemed like a change of subject, but perhaps thinking of her daughter's future had reminded her of her own past. My look of surprise was enough to give Olivia my answer.

"I left when you did," she said quietly. "Moved to L.A."

"Why?" I asked with astonishment.

"Because of you, Ted."

Chapter 21

Fortunately, Baccala really was a restaurant for night owls, because Olivia's four-word answer began a conversation that lasted through dinner and launched us on a second bottle of champagne.

"After you left, I just couldn't stand being at Haviland any longer." She paused a moment before continuing. "I decided that if you could stand up to your parents and do what you really wanted, I could, too. I wanted to be an actress. Except for being with you, it was all I ever wanted. Once you were gone, it was all I had left."

She looked up, and our eyes met. Before I could respond, Olivia went on.

"My mother and I fought for weeks, but I finally convinced her to let me go and live with her parents in Van Nuys. I promised her I'd finish high school. I got my first job in a commercial just before I turned seventeen." Olivia fell silent, her fingers playing with the stem of her champagne flute. I just watched her, and at last she spoke again.

"Remember when we went to your parents' house that weekend?" Olivia continued.

My mind traveled back to the day we drove there, and that night! I'd never let myself think about those few ecstatic moments when we had held each other. The feelings flooded back to me as I remembered the bliss of our bodies touching, bringing at last into three dimensions the sweet connection we shared.

"I don't want to make it sound as though your parents treated me badly, but—"

"What did they do?" I asked, suddenly annoyed. "What did they say?"

Olivia took both my hands in hers.

"Teddy, it's okay. It was a long time ago." She paused. "I don't think your father realized how horrible I felt about my mother's leaky old station wagon. He told me it had permanently stained the flagstones on your driveway."

"He told you that?" I said, anger rising. "If I had known—"

Olivia touched my hand. "It doesn't matter now," she said, "but at the time it made the chasm between us so obvious. I tried to deny it, but you were a privileged rich kid, and I was the cleaning lady's daughter. I don't think your dad had any idea, but pointing out those oil spots did a better job of putting me in my place than any direct criticism ever could have."

"He knew exactly what he was doing," I said. "I'm so sorry. I wish I had known."

"It doesn't matter anymore," Olivia said, "and your mother was really very kind. She asked me what my dreams were, what I wanted more than anything. I said I wanted to be an actress, and she said there was no reason I couldn't be a fabulous one as long as I didn't get distracted. Then she asked me if I was an only child."

"What? Why?"

"She said that only children have special challenges because they don't have any siblings to take the spotlight off them and they have to carry the burden of their parents' expectations alone. She said she knew what she was talking about because she was an only child. And so are you, and so was your dad." Olivia paused. "She was right. Only children do have more to live up to."

"She was right about your acting ability. You're terrific."

Olivia sighed. "My acting was never better than during those last few weeks of school that year. After I told you things were over between us, pretending that they really were over took every molecule of acting ability I possessed. And your father—"

"My father did something else?" I asked, anger again rising inside me.

"Do you remember in the morning how he asked me if I wanted to see his gem collection? He showed me all the stones, and then he singled out one diamond. He said you had already picked that one out for—"

"What? I—" But Olivia went on.

"He said you'd chosen it for an engagement ring, and that you had a girl already picked out, too: the daughter of two of the dinner guests I'd met the night before. Karen. She was your childhood sweetheart, he said, and she was going to college in the East, just like you."

"Damn him!" I exclaimed a little too loudly. "And you know what makes me really angry? He did offer me that diamond to give to someone someday. But not to Karen! We were only friends because our parents were friends. I took her to a movie over Easter vacation because my parents practically ordered me to."

"I didn't believe him at first, but then—" Olivia bent her head down as she went on, speaking more softly. "But then you were just so—so *happy* after that, so excited about going to Juilliard. I couldn't help wondering about what your father said, and whenever I made up my mind to ask you about it, you were always talking nonstop about how wonderful everything was going to be."

Olivia looked into my eyes, and I saw the old pain there. She paused, then sighed deeply. "And then you lied to me."

"What?" My mind was reeling. "I never lied to you."

"You said you had to go home to have dinner with your aunt."

Stunned, I stared at Olivia as I struggled to remember—*damn!* She had known I didn't have an aunt. I *had* lied to her.

"I waited until *Camelot* was over so the show wouldn't suffer." She brushed a stray tendril of hair off her forehead, then continued. "I hoped against hope that you'd pursue me and insist that I take you back. I even would have felt better if you'd chased me down and cursed me, but—well, by the time graduation rolled around, I figured I was right. Your dad had told me the truth, and you were the liar."

We both just sat there for a few minutes. I tried to let the fury toward my father subside. Damn him! How could he have been so devious? Suddenly, I remembered something.

"I did lie about having an aunt, Olivia, but it wasn't because I had another girlfriend." I paused. "And what difference would it have made, anyway? You had another boyfriend."

"What?" Olivia seemed genuinely astonished.

"It's okay, Olivia. It was a long time ago."

"But, Ted! I don't know what you're talking about!"

"I saw you with him," I said. "The day I came back from the senior trip. A week before graduation. In the secret garden. Olivia, I saw him kiss you."

Olivia ran a hand through her hair as she thought back.

"Oh, my God, Ted," she said at last. "You're talking about Chuy! He and I went to the secret garden to talk. We wanted to get away from the grownups and little kids."

I sat silently until she continued.

"Chuy's my cousin. My dad's sister's son. He and his family

were visiting from Mexico. I hadn't seen them since I was little."
She laughed a little sad laugh. "It's weird that you saw us, Teddy.
I told him about you when we were sitting out there, and he tried
to cheer me up. He told me my dad would have wanted him to
look out for me. Chuy remembered my dad. He's almost six years
older than me."

"Your cousin. If I had only known."

"And you didn't have another girlfriend?"

I shook my head. "Not that my parents didn't want me to. My
mom made me go home that weekend to go to Karen's birthday party.
I didn't want to tell you because I thought you'd think I was dating
her."

"I thought you were practically engaged." Olivia smiled and
sighed. "Kids are so stupid. Always jumping to terrible conclusions
without enough to go on."

I looked at her as I thought back to those last days before graduation. "Wait a second!" I said. "Didn't you get my letter?"

Olivia didn't reply. She just pulled her shoulder bag into her lap
again, and opened it. She drew out an envelope and laid it on the
table between us.

"You mean this letter, Ted?" she asked, and I stared at the familiar
handwriting and stationary.

"Yes!" I said, astonished. Picking up the envelope, I slid the folded
page out from inside it. There, written in blue ballpoint pen, was the
message I had labored so hard to perfect so many years before.

I couldn't take my eyes off the careful handwriting. It took me
back to the day I wrote it, the day before I left for San Francisco on
the senior trip. I remembered how I'd slipped into the mailroom and
left it in Eleanor de la Vega's mailbox. Olivia didn't have her own
pigeonhole because she didn't live in the dorm.

"I got that letter yesterday," said Olivia, yanking me back to the present.

"Yesterday?"

"My mother sent it. She's the one who kept it all these years." Olivia took a breath and continued. "She's sorry now. She said she has regretted keeping that letter from me ever since I phoned her from Las Vegas to tell her that Jay and I had just gotten married. When I mentioned last week that I had seen the announcement of your concert in the *New York Times*, she told me she wanted to send me something. 'Don't hate me for this, Livie,' she said, 'I did it because I love you.' Three days later, your letter arrived."

God damn parents. Why can't they love their children just a little less?

A peculiar combination of emotions rumbled through me. I was angry at my father and at Eleanor de la Vega, and I was disgusted with myself for having failed to see through their machinations. I could have—I should have—but then a wave of euphoria enveloped me. Olivia and I were sitting across a table from each other! I gazed at her, awed that the old connection between us was still so undeniably present. It was as though no time had passed, not even a minute.

"Teddy," she said, "I would have been there."

"So this is our meeting, then," I said. "You got the letter, and we're talking. A couple of decades late, but here we are."

Our eyes met, and we both smiled. Nineteen years vanished as we sat entranced in the candlelight. How could that indescribable link still be there between us? How had I ever convinced myself that soul mates don't exist? I sat there in awe, amazed at the current coursing between us. I wanted to touch her, but I just sat there transfixed, lost in the astonishing wonder of it all.

"Did you play your violin outside one night, Ted?" Olivia asked suddenly. "The same piece you played at the folk music festival—and as your encore tonight?"

She knew I had played it for her!

I nodded. "Yeah, I did. In the secret garden. I had the crazy idea you might come to find me."

"But you stopped," she said. "Later, I thought I must have dreamed it."

I shrugged. "Mr. Gillespie found me and sent me back to the dorm," I said. I looked at her as I thought back to that night and how desperate I had felt. "He knew why I was there, Olivia. I still remember what he said."

"What?"

Our eyes locked, and I smiled.

"If it's real, it will survive."

As I looked at her, Olivia smiled, too. I hadn't believed the old guy all those years before, but damned if he wasn't right. The connection between Olivia and me was real. Through nineteen years of my unrelenting denial, it had survived.

Just then, a busboy began to mop the floor near our table.

"Olivia, this place is getting ready to shut down," I said. "Would you like to continue our conversation at my hotel? We can have a nightcap in the bar there."

The maître d' summoned a taxi for us, and we were soon walking into the Warwick.

"Couldn't we just go to your room, Ted?" Olivia asked. "I'll be able to relax better. The last thing I need right now is to have a picture of us together show up in a tabloid. Jay and I are on fairly good terms, and I want to keep it that way for Teddie's sake."

And just like that—like magic, really—Olivia and I were alone in my room on the thirty-second floor. The evening maid had visited, which meant the bed had been neatly turned down and a foil-wrapped chocolate rested on each pillow. The radio was tuned to a classical music station, filling the room with the strains of Schubert's Unfinished Symphony. I set my violin case on the coffee table and opened the drapes so we could admire the city lights below. Olivia joined me at the window as she took off her scarf, and for a few minutes we just stood there silently.

"You always said that someday we'd be in New York together," she said at last. "If I had believed you, maybe it would have happened sooner."

"It's happening now, and that's all that matters," I replied. "Nobody ever gets to know what might have been. Just like Schubert. We'll never know what he really had in mind for this symphony."

We moved closer together, and our shoulders touched. I moved my arm around Olivia's waist and rested my hand on her hip. The soft fabric of her dress slipped against her skin. I felt the warmth of her body against my fingertips.

How can I describe touching her again? It was so natural, so familiar. It was a feeling I knew by heart, and at the same moment so thrillingly new. Olivia reached her arm around my back and put her hand on my own hip. We stood there, our arms crossed over like two school chums.

"Schubert's gone, Teddy," Olivia said, "and you're right. We'll never know. But us—aren't we still a work in progress?"

Almost involuntarily, my arm tightened around her waist, and I felt my pulse quicken.

"We had a great overture—" I began, and the music seemed to envelop us. I turned at the same moment Olivia did. Her head was tipped a little forward, and I kissed her forehead. Then she looked up, smiling.

"We had a fantastic overture," she said, gazing into my eyes. "I'm dying to know how the rest of the symphony turns out."

Nineteen years vanished like a two-beat rest. I wrapped Olivia in my arms, and the first crescendo began.

Chapter 22

The night was a night of perfect timing, harmony, and splendor, like one of those rare performances when an orchestra plays with an inspiration like divine fire. Even our undressing seemed choreographed, an achingly beautiful ballet. I gazed at Olivia's supple form naked in the half-light, and no rush of self-consciousness rose within me as her eyes washed over my own body.

She shimmered golden, her dark hair falling to her breasts. I wanted to rush to her, to clasp her to me, to possess her, but the moment itself held me back. The energy between us was like a pure, clear note, and it gained in intensity as we stood there transfixed. Then, slowly, glidingly, she came to me, her hands touching my face, her nipples brushing my chest. Olivia was my Guenevere, and I was Lancelot again, her perfect knight.

I took her face in my hands, and my words seemed to come without my bidding. "I love you, Olivia," I said. "I always have. I always will." My lips on hers forbade her answer, but her body provided response enough.

We lay in each other's arms, exploring and discovering. I was hot with desire, but the symphony we were creating together was too ecstatic in its slow unfolding to rush to a conclusion. Her touch was electric, and my fingers, too, fairly sparked as I traced each contour of her body. She sighed as I touched and tasted and caressed, a sweet keening that echoed my longing and catapulted us both to a high wave of undulating joy.

At last we came together. At first, we moved gently, overwhelmed with the surging rapture of that long-awaited contact. And then it was all too much. We were wild together, lion and lioness, impatient in our hunger, voracious in our desire. At last, breathless and exhausted, we lay once again in each other's embrace.

I was still coasting drowsily in that intoxicating delirium when Olivia said something I couldn't quite hear.

"What?" I asked gently, stroking her hair. I loved the way it was spread out on my chest.

"*Coda*," she said. "Isn't that the word for when you've come to one ending, but it's not the real ending, so you get to have another one?"

I laughed. "Close enough, I guess," I said. "Why?"

Olivia pulled herself up on one elbow, kissed me, and grinned. "You really have to ask?"

Not anymore I didn't, and the music began all over again. The concert wasn't over until the sun crept in the window and reminded us that time wasn't standing still after all.

After breakfast, which we enjoyed while wrapped in fluffy white hotel bathrobes, we made a few plans. Olivia called the Plaza, checked her messages, and arranged for her luggage to be transferred to the Warwick.

"They've 'wrapped' the movie, Teddy," she said when she hung up. "Looks like I really am free. But I'll keep my suite at the Plaza as planned, until Sunday." She turned her green eyes on me and smiled. "Of course, if anyone really wants to find me, they'll have to look a little further."

Wonderful! I had nothing scheduled in Boston until the following Monday.

"Snow days," Olivia said. "Unexpected days off. They're better than finding a bag of money in the park."

Especially when there's no snow in sight, I thought. It was springtime in New York, and I had three days to spend with the woman I loved doing nothing but loving her more.

Olivia moved from the telephone to the sofa beside me. She stroked my hair and kissed me on the cheek. "It's your turn now, Teddy," she said. I smiled and kissed her back.

"No, I mean your turn to talk. You know about me and Teddie and Jay. What's happened in your life since the curtain came down on *Camelot*? Beyond the violin, I mean."

I knew what she was asking, and she had a perfect right. We were lovers now, both curious about what the future might hold.

"There's not much beyond the violin, Olivia," I said. "Sometimes I feel as though I'm married to it."

Olivia was silent, waiting for me to continue.

"My last year of college, I had a girlfriend, another violinist. It was a relationship of convenience, and it ended when we graduated. Then, when I first moved to Europe, I kind of fell together with another American, an oboe player from Baltimore. That lasted until she got a job in Chicago."

I paused, unsure of what to say about Valeria.

"There was one woman," I began at last. "An Italian soprano. We almost got married."

"What happened?"

I gazed at Olivia. "I could say she found another guy," I said, "but it was really my fault. At the time, I didn't know what kept me from making a commitment to her, but now—" I looked at Olivia. "I wanted her to be you."

"I never stopped loving you, Teddy," Olivia said. We were silent a moment.

"Jay was okay, though, at least at first," Olivia finally continued. "And he was a terrific manager. I just never felt about him the way I do about you. I kept telling myself that you were just a fairy tale, and I was just a child. I never completely convinced myself, but I did develop a kind of numbness."

Numbness. Without even knowing it, I'd cultivated the feeling myself. Until now, it had actually seemed normal to live my life in a half-dead state. Until now, when I could reach out and touch the face I had pretended to forget.

We never got past the bathrobe stage that day, never set foot outside the room. For the first time in nearly thirty years, I let a whole day go by without opening my violin case.

Chapter 23

Thinking about that other violin case makes me look again at the one sitting near me on the coffee table. I've closed the lid on the magnificent instrument it contains, but I can't close my heart. I know the price of numbness now, and it's more than I can pay. I'd rather weep than feel nothing. I'd rather suffer the pain than deny the truth that Olivia is lost to me again.

It's autumn in New York right now, but the whole world was engulfed in springtime those three idyllic days I spent with Olivia. The second day, we played tourist, a luxury I hadn't experienced since the days I'd spent with Albert van Doren when I came to New York for my audition at Juilliard. And Olivia had never had the opportunity at all, even though she had visited Manhattan a number of times.

"I've always been at the mercy of schedules and handlers," Olivia said. "I've never had the chance to 'trip the light fantastic,' and I've always wanted to ride on a New York subway."

Olivia tucked her hair inside a Yankees baseball cap and put on a pair of oversized sunglasses. Just to be on the safe side, I, too, wore dark glasses, but it was obvious after we took a cruise around Manhattan on the Circle Line that our anonymity was ensured. Nobody gave a damn about a pair of thirty-something lovebirds, even if one of them was carrying a violin.

It seemed obvious to both of us that our lives together had begun, that we were on a kind of advance honeymoon. Time and fate—and probably even our parents—were on our side at last, and it seemed as though nothing could divert us from "happily ever after." The only delay would be Olivia's divorce.

"The process has already begun," she explained over a glass of wine. We were sitting in the bar at The River Café, and the lights had just come up on the Brooklyn Bridge. "Jay and I have settled just about everything, even Teddie. We've agreed that she should continue living with me, and Jay will visit as often as he likes. Things won't be much different than they are now. He's a busy guy." Olivia stopped talking, thought a moment, and spoke again. "Teddie's going to love you, Teddy."

We both laughed at how silly it sounded, but even while I was still smiling, a hint of worry crept into my mind. What if Teddie didn't love me? What if she hated me? I looked at Olivia, and she already knew what I was thinking.

"It may take a while, Ted," she said. "But she will love you. You don't have to worry about that."

"How can you be so sure?" I said. "I can't even imagine what it's like to get a replacement father, just like that."

"You won't be a replacement," Olivia said, taking my hand and patting it. "You'll be an addition." She paused, and I gazed into her eyes while she chose her next words.

"Teddie is lucky," she said at last. "She'll have two dads." She paused and squeezed my hand. "It'll make up for the fact that I had none."

I smiled, realizing I was hearing the story she'd tell Teddie, and I was grateful that it comforted me as much as I believed it would please my new stepdaughter. No one was getting squeezed out, and if we were lucky, Jay would think so, too.

"It seems to me," Olivia went on, "that the question of where we'll live is a much more complicated issue. I really don't have the option of leaving L.A.—"

"No!" I said quickly. "It's simple! I've needed an excuse to leave the Vienna Phil for years now. I've been working on building a solo career, and I'm ready to take the final step. I can live anywhere, Olivia. Los Angeles is perfect. Do you know how happy it will make my mother?"

Olivia laughed. "I know how happy it will make me," she said.

And as we sat there, holding hands and looking out over that marvelously iconic skyline, I truly felt as though the gods were smiling on us.

But wait! Hadn't I felt like this before? A cloud passed in front of my blue-sky daydream as I remembered how my feelings had soared in those giddy weeks before *Camelot*. Could something go wrong this time, too? But I looked again at Olivia's happy face, and my anxiety vanished. We are older now, I told myself, no longer two idealistic children. We haven't set our hopes any higher than our love can carry us. Life always has its challenges, I knew, but now that we were together again, the challenges we faced seemed almost inconsequential.

The third day, we went to the Museum of Modern Art, but we were too wrapped up in each other to pay proper attention to its treasures. Our impending separation intensified our conversations and, later, our lovemaking. We lay awake in each other's arms until dawn, and never in my life has a rising sun been more unwelcome.

Was a wiser part of me aware even then that our passionately laid plans might come to naught? At the time, I thought it was only ordinary sadness that my perfect sojourn with Olivia was drawing to a close. Now, though, I wonder if I didn't know, somewhere in the depths of my consciousness, that a storm was lurking just beyond the tranquil horizon.

On Sunday morning, a bellman arrived for Olivia's luggage while we were still lingering over our coffee. Half an hour later, I accompanied her down to the lobby, where a taxi was waiting to take her to the Plaza. Although it was only a few blocks away, we had decided against walking there together. After preserving her anonymity successfully for three days, we'd have been foolish to run the risk of exposure at the last minute.

"The media knows my schedule," Olivia had explained. "When I leave for the airport, there won't be a shortage of photographers on hand, and I wouldn't put it past the determined ones to show up early and figure out who's lurking behind these shades. They could unmask Batman if you gave them half a chance."

Our good-bye was as short and abrupt as death by guillotine. One minute Olivia was standing next to me, and the next she was rolling up Avenue of the Americas in the back of a taxi. Suddenly I was alone again in New York City, unless you count the violin case I was clutching in my right hand.

Chapter 24

I began my season at Tanglewood with a happy confidence that Olivia and I would be together forever by Christmas. We talked on the phone almost daily. I'd call her each night before I went to bed, reaching her mid-evening. I never knew when she might call me, but I didn't mind being awakened at odd hours. It was all temporary, all happy. Except for what appeared to be the usual kinds of legal snags, Olivia's marriage seemed to be on a swift path to dissolution, and our long conversations confirmed what we had always known: We belonged together.

I called her the moment I heard the good news. "I'm coming to California," I said. "I've been invited to perform in San Francisco, just before I return to Vienna. I'll have a little over a week. We could—"

"God, Teddy," interrupted Olivia. "You know I'd love to see you, but the timing couldn't be worse. Jay is dragging his feet about our custody arrangement, and he's raising some other issues, too. If he finds out about us—"

I understood, I said, and I performed in California without even visiting my parents. I kept on "understanding" as my conversations with Olivia focused less on our plans for the future and more on the unhappy union she was trying to escape.

By November, the divorce attorneys had succeeded in turning a civilized breakup into a battle royal, and one story about the ugly proceedings even made it into the *International Herald Tribune*. Jay was arrested for breaking into Olivia's house and abducting Teddie. The charges were dropped, but Jay spent a night in jail.

Olivia suffered greatly through the ordeal. "It's exactly what I didn't want to happen," she told me again and again. "I never should have listened to my attorney when he told me to change the locks on my house. But he said, 'Do you have a key to *Jay's* place?' and like a fool, I let him whip up my emotions. Now Teddie has seen her father in handcuffs, and she's having trouble in school, and—"

"I have to see you," I said.

"Teddy, you know I can't—"

I had nothing to say, and at last Olivia spoke again.

"Jay will be in Chicago with his parents over Thanksgiving," she said quietly. "Maybe we could get together in New York again."

"I'll be there," I said. I'll take time off from the Phil, I told myself. In ten years, I'd never missed a performance, but Olivia was far more important than a perfect attendance record.

"We'll have to be careful," Olivia said. "I don't want Jay to—"

"Don't worry," I said. "I'll grow a beard and dye my hair blue. Or maybe I'll wear a zoot suit, so everyone will think my violin case has a machine gun in it."

At last Olivia laughed. "Oh, God, Ted," she said. "It'll be great to see you, and you can finally meet Teddie."

As our plans developed, it turned out I'd be seeing Eleanor, too. She loved the idea of taking Teddie to the Macy's Thanksgiving Day Parade, and she reminded Olivia that her babysitting services would come in very handy. I couldn't argue with the logic, but as the last weekend in November drew near, I found myself wishing I were meeting Olivia alone at the Plaza. I just didn't feel prepared to face a whole new family.

Teddie scared me the most. I still worried that she might see me as an evil interloper, someone who was preventing her parents from getting back together. I had no experience with children even under the best of circumstances. Would I act the right way, say the right things? All I could think was that I should greet my stepdaughter-to-be with a really wonderful gift.

"She's seven," I told the salesclerk at a toy store in Vienna. The woman showed me dolls dressed in elaborate costumes, stuffed animals, and even a little toy piano. Everything was lovely, but I couldn't decide. My present had to be perfect, and I had no idea what Teddie might like.

After the toy store failure, I thought about jewelry, and I almost bought a gold heart-shaped locket that reminded me of the one Olivia used to wear. What stopped me was the price. It was expensive, and even though I could easily afford it, I thought it would look like I was trying to buy my way into Teddie's affections.

I racked my brain, and suddenly I remembered the photograph of Teddie that Olivia had shown me. She was wearing a leotard and tutu. My mind traveled instantly to a music box my mother used to keep on her dressing table. It was covered in velveteen and it stood on four little gold claw feet. When you lifted the top, a little ballerina popped up and twirled to a tinny rendition of "Für Elise."

"My father gave me this when I was a little girl," she used to tell me. "It was the best birthday present I ever got."

It took a full day to find it, but the moment I saw it, I knew my search had been worth the effort. The box was finished in pale robin's egg blue enamel and was topped with a delicate pair of gold ballet slippers. When I turned the key and raised the lid, a tiny porcelain ballerina pirouetted in front of a mirror to the "Dance of the Sugarplum Fairy." The music box was nothing like the inexpensive child's toy my mother had loved. This one was as beautiful as a Fabergé Easter egg, and it cost three times as much as the locket I'd deemed too expensive. I bought it immediately.

As perfect as it seemed to be, my gift for Teddie did little to settle my nerves as I counted the days until my trip to New York. What if she hated me on sight? What if I hated *her*? Eleanor worried me, too. It was encouraging that she had sent Olivia my ancient letter, but what if I didn't measure up to her memories and expectations when she saw me after all these years? All the while wishing that I could have one more rendezvous with Olivia before I met my future mother-in-law, I decided I'd bring Eleanor the biggest *Sachertorte* money could buy. I thought it was a safe guess that Eleanor liked chocolate, and Vienna's most popular pastry came in a special wooden box that made it look like a treasure.

Once I had presents for her mother and her daughter, I realized I needed something for Olivia herself. My first thought was to take her the same kind of champagne we'd had at Baccala the night of our reunion. When I realized that such a present would be as much for my own enjoyment as hers, I arranged to have roses waiting in her room instead.

None of these preparations took nearly enough time to keep me from fretting all through November. By the time I boarded my Lufthansa flight to Frankfurt and New York, I had imagined every possible scenario, including one that arrived in the form of a nightmare. I dreamed that Jay appeared while we were eating Thanksgiving dinner, and right there in the restaurant, he pulled a gun. I woke up in a drenching sweat, my heart pounding fiercely. Guenevere needed Lancelot more than ever, but could Ted Spencer rise to the challenge?

Chapter 25

Only now am I willing to admit to myself that Olivia didn't need a white knight to rescue her from her marriage any more than she had needed one to whisk her away from life in a housekeeper's cottage back in high school. It's just the story I've told myself all this time, a story that cast me not only as selfless and noble, but also as the perfect new stepfather, son-in-law, husband, and lover. Weren't my carefully selected gifts irrefutable evidence?

"It's not enough." That's what Olivia said tonight when I told her the Merino Rose was far too large a gift for me to accept. "It's not enough, but it's what I have to give."

It's taken me fourteen years, Olivia, but at last I understand. Presents are only tokens, no matter how much you spend on them. The only reason I'm glad I have the Merino Rose is that you brought it here yourself. The only way it could ever make me happy is if you'd stayed.

The bellman had just left my room when the telephone rang.

"Teddy! It's me!"

"Olivia! Where are you?"

"Room 927. Why don't you come on up?"

"I asked if you'd checked in when I got here, but—"

"I'm sorry. I should have told you I register under a phony name these days. I've been here since a little after one." It was nearly seven now. My plane was half an hour late, and traffic had been a nightmare.

"I'll be right there."

The bellman had filled my ice bucket, and I took a few moments to dig the bottle of Veuve Clicquot out of my bag and start it chilling. Then I picked up my violin and headed for the ninth floor.

When Olivia opened the door, she was holding the telephone receiver up to her ear. I set my violin case on the dresser and slipped off my leather jacket as she finished her conversation.

"No, Jacob," she said emphatically. "I don't care. That's how it's going to be. Listen, I've got to run, but I'll call you in the morning."

After she hung up, she turned toward me. She was smiling, but her face was pale. I had the fleeting thought that she might have been crying.

"Teddy," she said. "I'm so glad to see you."

I didn't say anything as she fell into my arms. I just held her, kissed her hair, breathed her in. Suddenly Olivia pulled away.

"I'm alone," she said, and I smiled. I'd have her to myself for a little while before—

"No, I mean I'm here alone. Teddie and my mom didn't come."

"Why? What happened?"

"Oh, God, Ted," Olivia said, running both hands through her hair. "I don't know how, but Jay found out I was bringing Teddie here. He showed up just as we were leaving for the airport. To keep the peace, Mom stayed home with Teddie. So here I am. Not exactly what I had in mind, but—"

I didn't know what to say. I'd been dreading my first meeting with

Teddie, and now it wasn't going to happen after all. Why didn't it feel like good news?

"That was my lawyer on the phone," Olivia went on. "Jay's making it sound like I was trying to take Teddie out of state to hide her from him. It's ridiculous, but all's fair in war, I guess."

"Olivia, I'm sorry," I said lamely.

"Not your fault, Ted. Not your fault."

"So—?"

"So what's going to happen?" Olivia finished my question. "God, I don't know. I'll have to go back tomorrow, but we still have tonight to ourselves."

She was only partly right. We were together, which was what I had dreamed about for the last six months. But Olivia had to change her plane reservations, and her lawyer called again with a few more questions about Jay's latest gambit. Then, just when it seemed as though we'd reached a moment of uninterrupted silence, Eleanor called. Teddie was upset, and Olivia spent half an hour reassuring both of them she'd be back tomorrow in time for a late Thanksgiving dinner. The whole time, I just sat there, wishing we really were alone instead of trapped inside Olivia's toxic marriage.

"Thanks for the roses, Teddy," Olivia said when she finally got off the phone. "They're beautiful."

I looked at the red long stems in a glass vase next to the bed and nodded. They reminded me of the champagne I'd put on ice in my room. I should go get it, I thought, but somehow this didn't feel like a celebration.

"What do you want to do about dinner?" I asked.

"Why don't we just order room service?" Olivia said.

The phone rang again while I was looking at the menu. It was Eleanor, and Olivia spent another fifteen minutes explaining where to find Teddie's cough medicine and how to turn off the outdoor lights.

"I chose that house because I wanted Mom to live with us," Olivia said when she hung up. "It has the most perfect guesthouse, but—" She paused and looked at me. "She doesn't like Jay, and she's made a point of never making herself at home in what she thinks of as 'his house.' God, it makes me so mad. It isn't Jay's house. It's *my* house." Olivia sighed heavily, and I moved to the phone.

"Is chicken okay with you?" I asked.

"Whatever you want, Ted."

The phone rang just as I was reaching for the receiver, and Olivia rushed to pick it up.

"Jay!" she said.

I fled.

Chapter 26

I was fifteen feet down the hall before I remembered my violin. I'll go to my room and get the champagne, I told myself as I picked up speed. And then I'll go right back. I had never forgotten my violin before, and the thought of losing it made beads of sweat pop out on my forehead. I was practically running when I reached the elevator, and I probably would have made a dash for the stairwell if it hadn't been standing open.

Why am I so upset? I asked myself as the elevator descended two floors far too slowly. My violin wasn't going anywhere, and Olivia had a right to talk to her husband. I knew before she came that things were getting nasty. She didn't even want to come. She was here only because I insisted, and she got on the plane even though Teddie and Eleanor had to stay behind. It would have been perfectly understandable if she had cancelled altogether.

By the time I was in my room, I was calm enough to call room service and order dinner for two to be sent to room 927. Then I retrieved the boxes containing the enamel music box and the *Sachertorte* from my suitcase, toweled off the champagne bottle, and headed once again for the elevator. When Olivia answered my knock, she smiled.

"I'm sorry, Ted," she said, and she kissed my cheek. "I know this is rough on you."

"I'm the one who owes an apology," I said. "I can't begin to know what it's like to—"

"Shh. Come on," she said, taking my hand. "We've got the evening to ourselves now. I told the desk to hold all my calls unless it's—"

"Teddie," I said.

"Yup. Teddies get to interrupt."

I smiled and felt my shoulders loosen.

"I brought champagne," I said, holding up the bottle. "I brought things for Teddie and Eleanor, too."

I set everything down next to my violin case. Olivia found two glasses, and I popped the cork.

"To us," she said, clinking her glass against mine, "and a happier future."

We both drank, and I set my glass down on the dresser.

"I brought your mom a *Sachertorte*," I said, picking up the wooden box and opening the lid. "Maybe you can have it for dessert tomorrow night. Have you ever had it before?"

"Never," Olivia said. She leaned forward to breathe in the aroma of dark chocolate. "Mom will love this. She's been a chocolate junkie for as long as I can remember. Teddie's not a big fan, though."

"That's okay. I have something better for her, anyway," I said. Opening the other box and removing the top layer of excelsior, I carefully lifted out the music box.

"It's from France, but I bought it in Vienna," I said.

"Ted! It's a work of art!" Olivia ran her fingers over the iridescent enamel and gold filigree. I set the box on the dresser.

"Turn the key," I said.

Olivia opened the lid, Tchaikovsky tinkled forth, and the little porcelain ballerina began to twirl.

"Ted, it's too much—" Olivia began.

"Do you think she'll like it?" I interrupted.

"It's absolutely gorgeous." Olivia closed the lid. "You spent too much."

There was a knock on the door, and soon dinner was set up in front of the window.

After all that had gone before, it seemed almost unbelievable that Olivia and I were alone in the room at last. We sat for a while across from each other, linen napkins in our laps and candlelight dancing on our faces. But soon, dinner forgotten, we moved to the sofa and snuggled together. As we held each other and talked, I couldn't help thinking back to the old beanbag chair in Bill Cross's light booth. Olivia and I were soul mates again, understanding each other almost without words.

"You're always with me, Ted," Olivia said, stroking my hair. "And I owe you everything I have. You're the one who taught me how to stand up for myself."

"I owe you everything, Olivia," I said. "You always expected the best of me. In *Camelot*. At the music festival in Santa Barbara."

"Uncle Chase was pretty hard on you," Olivia said.

"I could have blown him off, Olivia," I said. "It was you who wouldn't let me off the hook that day. You were the best music teacher I ever had." I kissed her.

"I'm no music teacher," she said.

"You're right," I replied. "You are my muse."

Olivia laughed and stood up. She stretched out her arms and spun around.

"I like the idea of being a muse," she said, and she reached her hand toward me. "But tonight—" I stood up, moved close, and kissed the top of her head. She unbuttoned the top two buttons of my shirt and laid her cheek on my chest. "For once, we're not phantoms and dreams."

She unbuttoned another button.

"Tonight we're just plain old earthbound bodies."

I laughed. "Plain? Old? Speak for yourself!"

But Olivia was done talking. Silently we undressed each other, touching and caressing until we stood together naked. When I took her face in my hands and kissed her, I tasted tears.

"Are you okay?" I asked.

She nodded, silent for a moment. Then she turned her face up to mine, and tears welled in my own eyes when she spoke.

"I'm never happier than when I'm in your arms."

All night long, we were the only people in the universe. The telephone remained miraculously mute as we made love, talked, then made love some more. All bitterness vanished in the presence of unutterable sweetness, and for one more perfect night, Olivia and I were one.

Chapter 27

We awoke in each other's arms. Wintry sunlight streamed through a narrow slit in the drapes. I had no idea what time it was, and I didn't care. Olivia was breathing rhythmically against my chest, and the only thing wrong in the world was that she had a plane to catch, and I had three more days in New York without her.

But not the rest of my life, I reminded myself. Soon everything would be resolved, and we'd be together for good. That last thought must have made me tighten my arms around her, because Olivia stirred and moaned in her sleep.

"Teddy?" she said.

"I'm here."

"I wish I didn't have to go."

"It's okay. This will all be over soon."

"Not soon enough."

Later, we had breakfast by the window, and as we ate I thought about the marching bands and the big balloons making their way along the parade route. It looked cold outside, but I couldn't help wishing I was out there, maybe even holding Teddie's hand.

"Ted," Olivia said, shaking me out of my thoughts. "The music box you brought Teddie is beautiful. I really wish you hadn't spent so much."

"It was important to me," I said. "It took me a long time to find it, and it seemed so perfect."

"It is perfect. Too perfect."

"What do you mean, *too perfect*?"

"I wish I didn't have to tell you this." Olivia looked away from me, out the window. The white sunlight lit her face and two tears that were standing in her eyes. She shook her head and looked at me again. "Teddy, I can't give her the music box. It wouldn't be fair to you."

"What are you talking about?"

"You hit the nail on the head when you picked it out for her, but—" Olivia reached across the table and took my hands in hers. "Teddie already has a ballerina music box that plays a tune. It's her most prized possession. Every night, I wind it up for her, and she falls asleep to the theme from *Love Story*."

"Why can't she have two?" I asked.

Olivia was silent for a moment. "Because Jay gave her the one she has. And it's not nearly as nice as yours. It's just a cheap little—" Her voice trailed off.

I pulled my hands from hers and pushed my chair back. I couldn't put a label on the feelings that were rushing through me. I had brought the perfect gift, and it still wasn't good enough. The longer I stood there, staring at the box that held the present Teddie would never receive, the more confused and angry I became. When the phone rang, it gave me an easy excuse to grab my violin case and leave.

I headed down the hall, but I slowed down before I got to the elevator. I can't keep running away every time the going gets a little tough, I told myself. It's only a music box, after all, and someday, when the war is over, I'll have a chance to give it to Teddie myself. I headed back to Olivia's room, ready to apologize.

Olivia answered the door with the phone to her ear, but as soon as I was in the room, she ended her conversation and hung up.

"I'm glad you're back, Ted," she said.

"I'm sorry I left."

"That was my lawyer on the phone." Olivia looked at me, and it was easy to see that whatever he'd called to tell her wasn't happy news. "Jay's making things very tough."

"He wants Teddie?" I asked.

"Good question."

"What do you mean?"

Olivia sat down on the edge of the bed and looked toward the window. "I'm not sure, Ted," she said. "I'm not sure."

I set my violin back down on the dresser and turned to face her.

Olivia's green eyes bore into mine. "You've always had money, Ted."

"What does that have to do with anything?"

"I've worked hard for everything I have," Olivia said, "and now Jay wants to take it all away."

"That's the deal?" I asked. "You get Teddie if you give him everything else?"

"He's been careful not to put it that way, but—"

"Just do it," I said.

"What?"

"Just do it. Give it to him. Take Teddie."

Olivia was staring at me now, and I couldn't read the feelings behind her eyes. Then she stood up, walked over to the dresser, and picked up my violin case.

"Would you let someone take this away from you?" she asked.

"You know it's not the same thing," I said.

"How is it different?"

"It's who I am, Olivia. It's what I do."

"It's your life."

"It's my career."

"That's what Jay wants to take away from me. He wants all the proceeds from everything I did while we were married. All the residuals, too."

There was nothing left to say, but there was no time left for talking anyway. It was already eleven, and Olivia's plane left Kennedy at two.

"I promise this will all be over soon, Teddy," Olivia said before she vanished through the departure gate. "All I'm asking for is a little more time."

Chapter 28

A blizzard swept across Europe two days before Christmas that year. When the storm subsided into a quiet freeze, Vienna was cloaked in a giant snowdrift. As a favor to a colleague, I had agreed to take his place in an ensemble for a vespers service in St. Stephen's Cathedral on Christmas Eve.

I was doing my best to ignore the holidays, a difficult task in a country that revels so thoroughly in Yuletide. Even though I fought to ignore it, the hectic Christmas cheer reminded me too much how slowly and painfully things were going for Olivia and me. Nothing had changed since we parted at Kennedy Airport at Thanksgiving, and as her battle with Jay dragged on, I wondered why she was fighting so bitterly over what had happened in the past. Jay couldn't take her future career, and he really didn't want their daughter. I found it harder and harder to understand why Olivia found it impossible to walk away.

After the service, I watched the cavernous nave of the cathedral begin to empty out. Wrapped in fur coats and face-concealing mufflers, family groups were leaving arm in arm to make their way home to celebrate in the warmth of glowing hearths and candlelit trees. I, on the other hand, would be returning to a dark and empty flat. I hadn't even thought about what I'd eat the next day, and suddenly it dawned on me that most restaurants would be closed. I'd probably end up in a deserted hotel dining room.

I was still lost in my dark thoughts when a smiling face framed in white fur moved in front of me, a woman I had never seen before.

"Edward Spencer?" she said with only a hint of German accent.

"Yes!" I replied, surprised. "I—"

"I am Sophie Reinhardt," she said, pushing back her hood and revealing a halo of blonde hair. "A friend of Karl Maurer." Karl was the one who had asked me to play for the vespers service.

"Oh, I—"

"Karl told me you have no family here in Vienna," she went on. "I, too, have found myself alone in the city for Christmas. I came to Vienna to attend the funeral of an old teacher of mine, and now the blizzard has delayed my return to Düsseldorf until after the holiday."

Pulling off a kid glove, she held her right hand out to me. I shook it, noting the strong Germanic grasp.

"Would you care to join me at my hotel for a glass of Christmas champagne?" she asked. "I know it is not traditional, but—"

I found myself fascinated by her perfect English, her precise pronunciation, her forthright confidence. Her firm handshake seemed to yank me out of my self-absorption, and I couldn't think of a single reason not to accept her invitation. Moving my violin case to my left hand, I offered her my right arm. Together we braved the cold for a few blocks on foot, and soon we were surrounded by the elegant warmth of the Hotel Sacher.

After depositing our coats with the cloakroom attendant, we made our way to a table in the bar. While Sophie consulted with a waiter about which champagne to order, I took stock of my unexpected companion.

Her pale blonde hair swirled in soft, unruly curls to her shoulders, a charming contrast to her precise aristocratic features. She was about my age, I estimated. Who was she? I wondered, and why had she sought me out? I looked again at Sophie, who met my gaze with confident blue-gray eyes.

"I have been wanting to meet you, Edward Spencer, ever since I heard you play Lalo's *Symphonie espagnole* here in Vienna. In 1985, I think."

"1984," I said, "but thank you."

If only things had been different. If only Sophie hadn't named my favorite violin piece. If she had been a little less capable, intelligent, and determined. If her hair hadn't floated around her face like spun gold. If her smile hadn't been so warm, or the weather so cold.

Chapter 29

With that first glass of champagne, I allowed myself to slide under Sophie's spell. Christmas wasn't a depressing disaster anymore, but a warm celebration in her suite at the Hotel Sacher. On Christmas day, we dined in front of a crackling fire on wild turkey stuffed with chestnuts, mashed potatoes, green beans, and cranberry sauce. When I expressed my surprise at the obviously American menu, Sophie smiled broadly.

"I hoped you would like it," she said. "The turkey was difficult, but the cranberry sauce was the real challenge."

The dinner was my first glimpse of Sophie's logistical talents, but it wasn't long before I realized I had involved myself with a woman who had the ability to get whatever she wanted. When she set her sights on me, did I really have the option of saying no?

Of course I did, but she was delightful and undemanding, and she helped me forget my pain. She didn't seem interested in words like "love" or "commitment." The daughter of a successful coal broker, she had education, culture, and money, and she dedicated her life to the projects she chose. My career was the project she'd most recently selected, and the results of her efforts were immediate. Within a few weeks of our first meeting, Sophie had arranged for me to give a solo concert at Wigmore Hall in London.

I was amazed when she called to tell me about it. Performing as a soloist at Wigmore Hall was something I had thought about—every violinist thinks about it—but I had never taken any steps to make it happen. Sophie, apparently through means no more complex than a phone call and a verbal handshake, had raised my budding solo career to a new level.

She laughed when I expressed my surprise on the phone.

"It was easy," she said. "Everything is easy when the time is right. I happened to call the day after Christina Neiswander cancelled. No one's doing you a favor, Edward. You're solving a problem for them."

And as much as I would like to deny it now, Sophie was solving a problem for me. If Olivia couldn't break things off with Jay the way she'd promised, why shouldn't I form an alliance with Sophie? It was only a business relationship and a platonic friendship, after all. Sophie was married.

Finding out that Sophie had a husband was a relief. I felt far more comfortable believing she was unavailable. But as the weeks passed, and Sophie came to visit more than once, I learned that her husband hadn't been part of her life for at least five years. They'd been separated since he moved to South Africa, where he worked for a German beer distribution company.

"I didn't want to leave Europe," Sophie said. "At first, Peter came back to Germany frequently, but it was just too far." She shrugged. "I suppose someday we will divorce, but our finances are already separate, and there are no children to worry about. Unless one of us wants to remarry, it really doesn't matter."

By the time my parents arrived in Vienna for a quick visit in March, there was no denying our liaison had grown more personal. Sophie spent most weekends with me, and it was obvious to anyone who came to my flat that she didn't stay at a hotel. We all went to dinner at a French restaurant downtown, and Sophie was eager to report on my blossoming solo career.

"We'll try to be there," my mother said when Sophie mentioned my concert in London, but my father remained silent. I knew he still hadn't completely forgiven me for choosing my own career, even after all these years. He didn't really wish me ill, but I knew beyond a doubt that my parents would not be in the audience at Wigmore Hall on the eighteenth of May. The only reason they were visiting me now was that it was an easy trip from Milan, where they had just attended a luggage show.

The August after our Christmas feast at the Sacher, nine months after I had last seen Olivia, I moved to Düsseldorf to live with Sophie in her many-windowed town house overlooking the Rhine. Sophie's gentle but inexorable encouragement had finally given me the confidence to leave the Vienna Philharmonic, and there was nothing to keep me in Austria.

I sent Olivia the news on a postcard I had bought for her months before, when our future together had still seemed possible. It had a picture of Franz Schubert on the front, and I had selected it to remind us of our own "Unfinished" Symphony.

> *Dear Olivia,*
> *I'm moving to Germany. I need a change, and I simply can't wait any longer for things to be sorted out between us. I'll call you when I know my new phone number, and I'll send my new address, too.*
> *I love you,*
> *Ted*

No one would consider that a terrible message, but it had no envelope. I realized the magnitude of my mistake the moment I dropped the card into a mailbox, but by then it was too late. Franz Schubert would arrive in Los Angeles bearing a message that could—and no doubt would—be read by dozens of prying eyes. Olivia would surely suffer, not only because of the message itself, but also because of what it implied. I had revealed our involvement and betrayed our secret affair. I could plead innocence, but in fact I had let my angry disappointment cause an injury that might never heal.

Meanwhile, Sophie made my life fresh and interesting. She woke up every morning with new ideas for promoting my career, and she worked tirelessly to make them happen. Before two years had passed, the former assistant concertmaster of the Vienna Philharmonic was an international star.

In October 1988, two months after I'd mailed the Judas postcard, I wrote to Olivia again, this time on stationery placed inside an envelope.

> *Dear Olivia,*
>
> *I hope this letter finds you and Teddie well. I am living in Düsseldorf now, and I wanted to send you my new address and telephone number. My solo career is really starting to flourish, and my schedule is keeping me hopping. I think about you often, Olivia, and I truly hope you are finding a path to happiness.*
>
> *Love,*
> *Ted*
> *Kaiser-Wilhelm-Ring 33*
> *Düsseldorf, West Germany*
> *Telephone: 49.211.161245*

She never called. She never wrote. Our long, hopeless love affair was over.

Chapter 30

Life was orderly and businesslike with Sophie, and I remember thinking that I would probably spend the rest of my life with her. Things could be a lot worse, I told myself. As a matter of fact, it was hard to see how things could be better. If we were more like business partners than passionate lovers, well, so be it. Life was a lot more peaceful than it would have been with Olivia, and the sex wasn't bad.

About a year after I moved to Düsseldorf, my mother telephoned to tell me that Bill Cross had called her.

"You two haven't done a very good job of keeping in touch," she said. "It's a good thing your father and I haven't moved."

It turned out that Bill knew I was living in Germany and he'd called my mother from Amsterdam to get my address. Three days later, I opened the front door and found myself face to face with my old buddy.

Bill didn't look much like a lawyer anymore. He was tan, for one thing, and his thinning hair was slightly sun bleached. He was still wiry, but now he looked muscular under his hibiscus-patterned sport shirt.

"Spencer!" he cried, throwing an arm around my neck. "It's been way too long!"

I had to laugh as he barged past me and began sizing up Sophie's town house. Suddenly, he was my old high school crony again.

"Damn, Spencer, you always land on your feet."

Bill crossed the polished hardwood floor and stood looking out the picture window over the Rhine. It was a perfect summer afternoon, which meant that all of Düsseldorf was out taking a stroll.

"I've always needed the ocean nearby to feel right," Bill said. "But a river like that—it might almost be enough."

He kept pacing while I poured two glasses of Mosel wine. Bill clinked his against mine when I handed it to him.

"To old friends," he said, but he didn't drink. He set the glass on the coffee table and started pacing again, stopping to stare at a Kandinsky watercolor hanging over the piano.

"Why are you here?" I asked, regretting my tone instantly. Bill laughed.

"Afraid I want to borrow money?"

"No, I just—" I began lamely.

"I know, Ted. You're curious. You're dying to know why I'm so tan."

At last Bill finished examining every piece of art in the room, and we sat down on the leather sofa facing the river.

"I'm gay, Ted," he said, taking a slug of wine. "Queer as a three-dollar bill." He looked at me, but I had no idea what to say. "Did you hear me? I'm a homo." I still had no clue how to respond, and we both just sat there for a long moment.

"Okay," I said at last, "but why are you so tan?" Bill's eyes met mine, and we both laughed.

"No more wife, no more corner office," he said. "Just a boat and a boyfriend."

Actually, the boat was a racing yacht that belonged to Craig Montegna, a client of Bill's old law firm. He was the general manager of a fancy steak house chain, and when he wasn't jetting around the world on business, he was sailing. Bill had given up his career in tax law when he moved into Craig's waterfront house on Balboa Island. He still did legal work when he felt like it, but he spent most of his time being Craig's first mate.

"Talk about landing on your feet," I said.

"Yeah," Bill said. "Looks like both of us have pulled gold rings. You're an international celebrity, and I'm a happy-go-lucky boy toy."

"So why are you here?" I asked again, but this time it didn't sound so harsh.

"Craig just opened a restaurant in Amsterdam, and he's scoping out Cologne," Bill said. "So that's why I'm in Europe. But I'm sitting on your sofa because I wanted to see whether fame has wrecked you." He took another hit of wine. "Has it?"

"Fame's a moving target," I said. "I don't feel famous."

"Do you think Olivia does?" Bill asked. I shrugged my shoulders. "Why do you ask?"

"She's the most famous person I know," Bill said. "Except I don't know her. Not anymore."

"I don't, either."

"But we sure did know her when." Bill jumped up from the sofa, walked to the window again, and began to sing. *"Don't let it be forgot, that once there was a spot, for one brief shining moment that was known as—"*

"Oh, please."

Bill turned, and the descending sun silhouetted him against the window. I couldn't see his face, only the black outline. "Where did we go wrong, Ted?" he asked.

"We didn't," I said. "This is as good as it gets."

"I never get to see my kids. I haven't seen my parents in years."

"But you and Craig—"

Bill laughed sadly. "The honeymoon's over. I'm just a guy in a gilded cage." He moved to the bar and refilled his wine glass. Carrying the bottle to the sofa, he sat down next to me. "More?" he asked, and I held out my glass.

"How did we get so many goodies and still end up screwed?" he asked.

"Speak for yourself," I said, but suddenly I couldn't bear the thought of Bill seeing Sophie and me together. He'd realize easily that I was just a guy in a nice cage, too.

"Let's go get drunk," I said, and Bill hooted.

"You got it, pal," he said, "but that should have been my line."

Late that night when Bill and I parted, we pledged once again to stay in touch. Once again, we didn't.

Chapter 31

A couple of months later, I came home one evening expecting to find an empty house. Sophie was meeting some old school friends for dinner, and I was planning to spend the evening catching up on correspondence.

As I hung up my jacket, I noticed a piece of paper lying on the side table in the entry hall. What could it be? I wondered. Sophie was the queen of tidiness, and she never left mail lying around in the open.

The page was creased from being folded in a business envelope. I flattened it out, and I didn't have to read very far to understand what it was. Sophie and Peter, the precise German prose declared, were legally divorced.

I stared at the paper in my hand, wondering why the news seemed to matter. I had never met Peter, and after Sophie first told me about his existence, she rarely spoke of him. Their marriage had been extinct for years, and Sophie herself said there was no reason for a divorce. Their finances had long been separate, and they had no children to consider, so—why now?

A slight rustle made me look up. Sophie was standing in the archway that led into the living room. She was clad in a bathrobe, and her hair was pulled back starkly from her face. I stared at her. Her eyes were red, and her makeup was smudged. Sophie never cries, I thought, but—

"Hello, Edward," she said softly.

"I … ," I began. "You—"

"Peter asked for a divorce a few months ago," she said. "He wants to get married."

I had no idea what to say. Why was Sophie so upset? For that matter, why was my own stomach in a knot? I laid the paper back on the table.

"I'm sorry," I said, not sure whether I was apologizing for reading her mail or expressing my condolences.

"Don't be sorry," she said. "Be happy. I'm free now." Tears streamed down her cheeks. I moved toward her, and as I put my arms around her, her shoulders shook.

"Don't cry, Sophie," was all I could think to say. "Don't cry."

We stood there silent for a few minutes. Gradually, Sophie's shoulders stopped quaking. She raised her face to mine.

"We're both free, Edward," she said.

"What do you mean?" I asked, my throat tightening.

"I mean we can get married."

I stared at her. Sophie had never mentioned marriage before. I had always assumed she wasn't interested in it, with me or anyone else. I looked away, then back, but Sophie wasn't giving me a way out. She had proposed, and she was waiting for an answer.

But what should it be? Was there any good reason not to marry her? Our life together was good. I liked and admired her; she had practically created my solo career; and we were terrific business partners. Why, then, couldn't I just say it?

Yes, Sophie! Nothing would give me greater happiness than to be your husband.

The words formed in my head, and I even opened my mouth. But maybe I just wasn't cut out for marriage. Whatever my failing, all I could do was stand there and watch clouds move across Sophie's face.

"It's all right, Edward," she said at last. "I already knew."

"No, wait," I said. "I'm just—I'm still surprised. Give me some time."

"No," Sophie said, shaking her head. "Consider my suggestion revoked. I've never been happy with less than a hundred percent."

"Sophie the perfectionist." I looked straight into her eyes, and I spoke before I could stop myself. "I love you, you know."

It was the first time I had ever said those words to her. I must have looked as shocked as I felt, because Sophie smiled.

"You chose the perfect time to tell me," she said.

She reached up and placed her hand on my cheek.

"I love you, too, Edward," she said, and then she paused, searching my face. Tears formed in her eyes, then spilled over. "But it's not enough, is it?"

Chapter 32

That summer I was in Toronto, where I was performing at Massey Hall. After my final bow, I returned to my dressing room. On the way, I passed Sophie, who was engaged in rapt conversation with Richard Schaumberg, a cellist with the Toronto Symphony Orchestra. He was younger than me by nearly a decade, and he was just beginning to get noticed in the international music world. My own first encounter with Sophie flashed before my eyes as I watched her take Richard's hand in her own.

Sophie didn't return to our hotel room until four the next morning, and later that day she informed me that she would be staying in Canada "for a week or two." I returned to Düsseldorf alone, and I immediately began to make plans to move back to the United States.

As I packed my things, I was amazed at how little I owned besides my clothing and my violin. A few boxes of books and files were all I had to ship. I didn't even own a car. I'd always driven one of Sophie's. It's almost as if I have only been camping here all this time, I thought to myself as I waited for the truck to take away my small stack of possessions. Almost as if I had never really moved in.

Just before I left Germany, Sophie sent me a telegram from Toronto to tell me that she and Richard Schaumberg were engaged. I was a little surprised that she had informed me of her plans by wire, but I quickly realized what her message really meant. I replied immediately to assure her that her house was already free of my presence, and that I had left my keys with her brother in Kaiserswerth.

Although my plan was to settle in New York, I decided I might as well visit my parents before embarking on a house hunt. My mother was delighted when I told her I'd be staying for a week. It had been at least a decade since I'd spent more than three consecutive days at the house on Mulholland Drive.

I arrived on a Wednesday, and Mom had made so many plans I felt like I was back in high school. She was most excited about the barbecue she had planned for Saturday night.

"The Halls are coming," she told me happily. "They live in Rancho Mirage now, but they're in town visiting Karen. Isn't it great that they're here when you are?"

"Karen's still got a husband, doesn't she?" I asked. She'd written me about her marriage to a UCLA philosophy professor about three years earlier, and I'd heard about the birth of twin daughters about a year after that.

"Of course," my mother said. "But Antoine won't be here. He's at a conference in Seattle."

Karen's daughters were tiny clones of her and each other. They had the same white-blonde hair she'd had as a child.

"Portia and Juliet?" I repeated when Karen told me their names.

"I'm still a huge Shakespeare fan," she said.

I sat down next to Karen on the edge of the blanket where the two little girls were busy with their dolls.

"They're beautiful," I said. "And you look great, too."

In fact, she did look good. She was wearing a white piqué sundress, and her hair had artful strawberry blonde highlights. She'd filled out a little, and I thought she looked happy, or at least content.

"Thanks, Ted," she said. "You look great, too." She looked at me, and I knew instantly she didn't mean it.

Just then, my father emerged from the house.

"Your dad loves the girls," Karen said as he headed toward us.

He plopped down on the blanket and twisted the lid off the small bottle he was holding. The little girls shrieked with glee as he surrounded them in a blizzard of iridescent bubbles.

The grandchildren he'll never have, I thought, and a wave of sadness washed over me as I sat there. My mother and Mrs. Hall were drinking white wine under the umbrella on the patio. Mr. Hall was setting up a croquet course on the lawn. I felt like Scrooge on a journey with the Ghost of Christmas Never. Wasn't this the way things should have been?

"I wish you could have met Antoine," Karen said, almost as though she had guessed what I was thinking.

"Is he your soul mate?" I asked.

Karen's smile faded into a look of surprise. "Don't tell me you still believe in bullshit like that, Ted." She paused. "I mean, it's okay when you're young and like to mope around wearing lots of black eyeliner, but—"

She patted my thigh and shot me a condescending smile. Gazing at me with unmistakable pity in her eyes, she said, "Having kids changes everything, Ted."

Just then, Portia or Juliet crawled over and climbed up onto her lap.

"Can you tell them apart?" I asked.

"In the dark with my eyes closed," Karen said. "But Antoine can't."

Chapter 33

Three days later I was in New York, and a few weeks after that, I moved into a co-op with a view of Central Park. I hired a new manager, and I continued to pursue the solo career Sophie had forged for me. Over the next several years, I also began to collect violins. As for my personal life, I once overheard a friend describe me as a "confirmed bachelor." It surprised me a little at the time, but I'm sure most observers would have agreed. I spent all my time tending my growing collection of instruments.

Expensive violins and their admirers reside in a small but global universe. As my collection grew, so did my involvement with connoisseurs around the world. It wasn't long before I was involved in appraising instruments for individual owners, prospective buyers, museums, and insurance companies. I played the role of broker in an increasing number of transactions, and I was often called upon for consulting services. Although I still performed regularly, this new vocation gradually took center stage in my life.

One Sunday night after I'd been living in New York for a couple of years, I turned on the television around eleven. I don't usually watch network news, but I wanted to find out the latest about a New York transit strike. I poured myself a brandy, and when I sat down to watch, I was glad that I had.

Filling the screen was the face of none other than my old friend Bill Cross. He was heavier, and he was completely bald, but I still would have recognized him without the caption: "Los Angeles Attorney William G. Cross," it read, "of Kenworthy, Steinmetz & Hobbs."

Bill was standing behind a bouquet of microphones, and one question rang out above the hubbub.

"Is it true you're having an affair with Mrs. de Soto?"

"Madeline de Soto is a friend and a client," Bill said. "We are confident that she will prevail against the absurd, vindictive, and frivolous action that the U.S. Attorney has brought against her."

Another salvo of questions immediately erupted, but the footage ended. The news anchorman summed up the latest skirmish in the ongoing De Soto scandals, but I had no interest in a New Age huckster on a kamikaze mission. She might be a boon to the tabloid trade, but as far as I was concerned, the sooner the nation was rid of her miracle-claiming health spas, her misleading infomercials, and her snake oil products, the better.

How could my old buddy be mixed up with an obvious bottom feeder like Madeline de Soto? I wondered as I jotted down the name of his law firm. But I couldn't help smiling. It was great to see him in action.

The next day, I called Kenworthy, Steinmetz & Hobbs. I didn't really expect Bill to be there, but I hoped he would call me back. To my surprise, the receptionist put me right through.

"Spencer! You dog!" Bill shouted.

"Has fame wrecked you?" I asked, and he laughed.

"Why didn't I see how great it is to be in the limelight when I was running that damn light booth? I should have been Lancelot myself."

"Why Madeline de Soto?" I asked. "Why aren't you saving the redwoods or something else that deserves it?"

"Maddie's got her flaws, but she's always paid her taxes," Bill said. "The Feds haven't been able to nail her for drugs or medical fraud, so they're trying to pull an Al Capone. She's being railroaded."

"How did she find an angel like you?" I asked.

"Oh, it was a friend-of-a-friend thing. One of them remembered some work I did for Kareem Abdul-Jabbar back when I was at Briscoe and Pitt and asked me to join her defense team. I never expected to get my picture in the tabloids, though. Or get linked to Madeline romantically. Ha! If they only knew!"

"Have you gone back into the closet or something?"

"No, but I'm on my own right now, and nobody's done any poking into my past. They will one of these days, and a whole new set of rumors will erupt."

"So how are you?" I finally asked. He sounded happier than I'd ever heard him.

"Good," he said. "My kids spend most weekends with me."

I caught him up on my own life, and before we hung up, we promised to keep in touch.

"I come to Los Angeles every couple of months," I said. "Let's at least have lunch."

"I come to New York sometimes, too," Bill said. "Let's get drunk."

Amazingly enough, Bill and I actually did get together the next time I went to L.A., and after Madeline de Soto's tax evasion charges were dropped, his role on her defense team made him a desirable speaker at conferences and trade shows. Such engagements brought him to New York several times a year, and he always found time to meet me for drinks or a meal.

"I guess I'm just not the type to have a 'significant other,'" Bill said one night over beers at McSorley's. "I always think I'm open to the possibility, but ... " his voice trailed off.

"I don't think I'm the type, either," I said.

Bill looked at me, and his face was suddenly serious.

"You're wrong, Ted," he said. "It's weird, but whenever I look at you, it's as though I should be seeing two people. Like you're a photograph with one face blacked out."

"What the hell are you talking about?"

"Olivia."

I stared at him. Why would he bring her up after all this time?

"You two had something."

"Yeah, we did. In high school."

"Are you telling me you never think about her?" Bill leaned forward and tapped his index finger on my chest. "I think about her every time I see you."

"I think about her," I admitted.

"Is that all you ever do?" Bill demanded. "Think?"

"She's married," I said. "Don't you read the papers?"

It had been impossible to ignore all the news coverage when Olivia announced her engagement to Arturo Ricciardi a couple of years before. He was a wealthy Italian nobleman old enough to be her father. The wedding made headlines on both sides of the Atlantic, not unlike when Grace Kelly tied the knot with Prince Rainier.

"Yeah," Bill said. "I know. And it's just wrong. You were supposed to marry her, you big jerk."

I couldn't bring myself to tell Bill about what had transpired between Olivia and me a few years before. I could hardly allow myself to recall those few blissful encounters and all I had done to ensure that none could ever follow. Only now can I think about it. Now that the Merino

Rose sits accusing me more relentlessly than Bill Cross ever could.

Old buddy, how could you read me so well? Was I such an open book to everyone but myself?

Chapter 34

The next time I saw Bill was in 1999, at my father's funeral. I had seen my dad only two weeks before, when he and my mother stayed overnight on their way home from Scotland. Having long since turned the reins of Spencer Luggage over to a new management team, my father had been pursuing his retirement vigorously on glamorous golf courses around the world. He was back on familiar turf at the Beverly Hills Country Club when he suffered a massive heart attack and succumbed before reaching a hospital.

The next night, as I lay on my boyhood bed, I pondered my mother's suggestion that I live in the house on Mulholland Drive. "It's yours now, Ted," she'd said. "It's too much for me now and I know Dad would be pleased if you carried on here."

Would he? I'd never know. Things were never the same between us after I refused to become part of Spencer Luggage. Although my father hadn't ignored my career, the feeling that I was a permanent disappointment had never left me.

I slept fitfully. Before dawn, I wrapped myself in a terry cloth robe, descended the curving staircase to the entryway, and passed through the living room on my way to the kitchen. The smell of Marlboros lingered in the air. The old man had never succeeded in giving up smoking, even though he'd tried countless times.

"I'll die with a cigarette in my mouth," he used to say, and he was very nearly right. He was about to light up after the fourteenth hole when he collapsed.

After making myself a cup of coffee, I walked through the rest of the house. I passed the guest room where Olivia had stayed, and the bath where we had embraced that night so long ago. When I reached my father's study, I sat down in the leather wing chair facing his rosewood desk.

The room was dim, and I could almost see him sitting across from me, hands folded, waiting for me to speak. But what was there to say? The only thing left of him was the scent of tobacco. I sat there in silence as the first rays of daylight stole around the edges of the drapes and raked across the big desk.

Suddenly I felt a hand on my shoulder, and I turned to find my mother standing behind me.

"I didn't mean to startle you, Ted," she said.

"I couldn't sleep."

"I haven't slept much, either, these last few days."

I stood and moved to face her.

"Mom, I'm so sorry," I said, kissing her cheek. She looked so pale, so tired.

"He loved you," she said.

"I know."

"I'm not sure you do." My mother moved to a bookcase directly behind the big desk. Pulling out two thick albums, she opened one, revealing page after page of carefully preserved newspaper and magazine clippings: *Time, Newsweek, Harper's, Esquire, The New York Times*. And there were programs, too, from Vienna, London, San Francisco, Sydney. But how—?

"He didn't always tell you he was in the audience, Ted." My mother had moved to the stereo now, and I stared at her as my own rendition of Saint-Saëns's Violin Concerto no. 3 filled the room. It was a piece I had mastered as a boy and still loved for its charming tenderness.

"He never listened to anyone else," she said. "Only you."

I was silent—what was there to say? My mother vanished down the hall, and I sat down again, facing my father's vacant chair.

The music rose around me, punishing me with its sweetness. If you loved me, Dad, why didn't you tell me? And why wasn't your heart big enough to hold Olivia, too? You should have been playing with your grandchildren these last few years, not gadding about exotic golf courses.

Despair slowly quelled my anger as the concerto's final strains engulfed me. I could rage against my father's stony silence, but I couldn't deny my own. I could play my violin all night long, but when it came to love, I was mute. My feelings were like forgotten sheet music, notes on a page with no voice to express them.

And now it was too late. He was gone, as utterly as my childhood, as incontrovertibly as a lifetime without Olivia. I sat there as the sun slowly illuminated his big empty chair, and I wept.

Chapter 35

My mother decided to move to a condo in Newport Beach that she and my father had purchased a few years earlier. When I came to visit her a month after the funeral, she was suffering greatly as she tried to choose the few belongings she would have room for in the smaller space.

"My mind knows it's time to set all this free," she said, running her hand over the piano in the living room, "but my heart can't get used to the idea."

I told Bill Cross what Mom had said over lunch in Venice, where Bill was pursuing a slightly Bohemian lifestyle in a small condo near the beach.

"I don't blame her," he said. "I have fond feelings for your parents' stuff, too." He looked at me thoughtfully. "Especially that big brown leather recliner in the family room. Is it still there? Did it survive all the manhandling I gave it back in high school?"

I smiled as I remembered the nights we'd stayed up late watching old horror movies on television. Bill always claimed the recliner.

"Yeah," I said. "It's there."

"I liked the guest room I always stayed in, too," he continued. "Your mom always put a special pillowcase embroidered with flowers on my pillow. 'Those are sweet williams,' she always reminded me, 'just like you.' I'll never forget that."

Bill's room was the same one where Olivia had stayed the one and only time she'd visited. I shook my head, trying to dispel the memory of that night.

"It's only stuff," I said.

"Yep. Just like your violins."

I looked at Bill, expecting to find the usual sly expression. But this time he only looked pensive, almost sad.

"Strings," he said. "So thin, and yet so difficult to sever."

Just before I left to catch a plane home, I took my mother's hand in mine.

"I'm too much of a New Yorker to live in Los Angeles, Mom, but don't get rid of anything just yet."

She looked at me, tears filling her eyes.

"I'm going to buy a house, Mom," I said, blinking to hide my own emotion. "In Connecticut, I think. It'll be big enough to hold all our furniture, and beautiful enough for you to love it. I hope you'll visit often and stay as long as you like."

Within six weeks, I'd found a homestead worthy of my parents' furnishings—not in Connecticut, but in Westchester County. A three-story colonial, the house has four fireplaces, eight bedrooms, countless shuttered windows, and a big red front door. It's in Sleepy Hollow, a town known for headless horsemen and my neighbor to the west, whose last name is Rockefeller.

Laugh if you will at the thought of a middle-aged bachelor living alone in eighteen rooms. If it elevates me to the ranks of the truly eccentric, so be it. All I know is that I've been at peace here. My mother comes to visit every month or so, and she relaxes among the familiar furnishings. Having failed to provide her with grandchildren, the least I could do was preserve the household she and my father created.

Several days ago, I made a trip to Westchester Airport to see my mother off. When I returned home mid-morning, I made a cup of coffee and sat down at my computer in the study. From my desk, I have a view through the maple trees beyond my driveway down to Hanford Road. I love that view and how it changes through the seasons. I especially love it now, as autumn breezes begin to bear away the rusty leaves.

When I sit here, no one can reach my door without my notice. I am not protected, however, from surprises that arrive through that other portal I've recently grown so dependent upon: the Internet. As I sipped my coffee, a message flickered onto my screen from an unfamiliar sender. Thinking it was yet another unbidden solicitation from a mortgage broker or a software vendor, I very nearly hit the "delete" key without reading the attached message. I was immediately grateful that my trigger finger was slow. The letter was from someone no keystroke could ever erase.

> *Dear Ted,*
>
> *It's been so long. How are you these days? And I might as well follow that with another question to which I'm embarrassed I don't know the answer. Where are you these days?*
>
> *I'm in Malibu. I bought a house here a few months ago, and my mother lives here with me. Teddie's off being a grown-up now— studying theater at UCLA and living in a condo in Westwood.*
>
> *You may well be wondering why I'm writing after all these years, and I think you'll find the reason ironic if you can bear with me through the long story.*

I don't know whether you know about my marriage ten years ago to Arturo Ricciardi. I met him when he was living in Los Angeles, and during our years together we spent quite a bit of time at his villa in Italy just north of Florence. Arturo died there almost exactly a year ago.

I loved him, Ted, and he loved me. Lots of people thought I could only be interested in someone so much older because he had money. But I have enough money, and I didn't need his. I made him promise to leave his estate to his six children before I accepted his marriage proposal.

No one was more surprised than I to discover that my name appeared in Arturo's will. He kept his promise about money and real estate and stocks and bonds, but he bequeathed me the entire contents of his study. It was a room where we had spent a lot of time together, especially toward the end, when his health was failing. I couldn't believe the bequest would be taken literally, but two months ago, the crates started arriving at my house in Malibu.

It's all here now: four Persian carpets, an inlaid mahogany armoire, two massive chairs, hundreds of books, a dozen paintings, three bronze statuettes, marble bookends, a Tiffany lamp, an antique French desk, a collection of meerschaum pipes, three Mont Blanc pens, a crystal inkwell—you just can't believe it. Even the overhead light fixture and an umbrella stand upholstered in ostrich leather.

My insurance agent has been helping me get everything appraised, because some of the items are museum pieces, and I feel I owe it to Arturo to take proper care of them.

This afternoon, when an appraiser was examining a teakwood chest, he discovered a compartment behind a false wall. Packed tightly inside was a violin wrapped in wool batting and foam rubber. It surprised me, because I'd never seen it before, and Arturo didn't play. It's in beautiful condition, and apparently quite old. The label inside reads: 'Joseph Guarnerius fecit Cremonae anno 1742 IHS.' I wish I could tell you it says 'Stradivarius,' but more than likely, it's a violin Arturo played as a child.

And now for the irony. I just sat down at my computer to check my e-mail before going to bed. On impulse, I typed the words 'violin appraiser' into a search engine. I didn't really expect to find anything useful, and I certainly didn't expect to find anyone I knew. But there you were, and your e-mail address was only a couple of clicks away. Kismet.

Ted, would you be willing to take a look at this violin? You'd be doing an old friend a great favor.

Yours,

Olivia

Chapter 36

I don't know which was more surprising, the letter from Olivia or the words on the label she had transcribed within it. Joseph Guarnerius "del Gesu" may not be the household name Stradivarius is, but there are many who prefer the instruments he crafted at his Cremona workshop. A label is no guarantee of authenticity, of course, but this violin had emerged from the estate of an Italian nobleman. Arturo Ricciardi was not only worth millions, he had roots back to the Caesars.

I wrote back immediately, and I found myself breathless as I typed.

> *Dear Olivia,*
>
> *It is wonderful to hear from you. Please accept my sincere condolences on your loss of Arturo.*
>
> *I am living just north of New York City in Westchester County— Sleepy Hollow to be precise. As you discovered when you searched the Internet, I have indeed become a violin collector, appraiser, and broker.*
>
> *If you say the word, I'll be on a plane to Los Angeles. Your violin may well be something very special, and I would be honored to assist you in any way I can to establish its provenance.*

Yours truly,

Ted

(914) 593-8941

"Sincere condolences!" "Yours truly!" I hated the triteness of those words even as I gave the command to send them. "I would be honored" was awful, too, especially since "ecstatic and terrified" were closer to the truth.

And it wasn't the violin that was making my forehead damp. As exciting as a rare instrument can be, not one has ever increased my heart rate. It was Olivia. Foolishly, I had begun to believe over the years that my feelings for Olivia had faded. Time and distance had allowed me to lull myself into thinking she was nothing more than a memory.

What an idiot I was to think I'd excised Olivia from my soul. Emotion tore through me like a flash flood in a narrow canyon. I shoved my chair back and spun around to rise. As I did, my elbow caught my coffee mug and sent it flying. It smashed as it hit the hardwood floor, exploding coffee and ceramic shards. Yo Yo, who had been dozing in the bay window, leapt to his feet with an outraged yowl and stalked out of the room.

It took me fifteen minutes to clean up the mess, and just as I sat back down at my desk, the phone rang.

"Ted? It's Olivia."

So soon?

"I just read your e-mail," she said. "Thanks for writing back so promptly."

I glanced at my watch. Eleven o'clock, which made it eight in L.A.

"It was great to hear from you, Olivia. It's—it's been too long."

A pause on the other end of the line. Was she still angry with me?

"It has been a long time, Ted. A lifetime in some ways."

Now it was my turn to pause.

"Thanks for offering to help me with this violin."

"I can be there tomorrow night, Olivia."

"No! I mean—I'd rather come to you."

"Oh. Well, okay, but really, I'd be happy to—"

"I'll come there. Is Wednesday all right?"

Wednesday was two days away, and I had nothing out of the ordinary planned. I agreed, and after I'd given Olivia my address—she refused my offer to pick her up at the airport—I gave her some pointers for keeping the violin safe while traveling.

"I'll see you Wednesday night, Ted," she said just before hanging up. "There's a flight that gets into Kennedy around five. Thanks again for helping me out."

I sat silent for at least ten minutes, though my mind was anything but quiet. Olivia had been brief and businesslike. All she seemed to want was a free violin appraisal. But if that were the case, why was she coming all the way to New York, and why had she insisted on making the journey all the way to my house? When I'd offered to meet her at the airport or at a hotel in the city, she told me she would be renting a car anyway.

"It really will be easiest if I come to your place," she'd said.

Her plan left me with nothing to do but sit tight for two days and answer the door when she arrived. What could be easier?

Playing a violin with boxing gloves on! My comfortable complacency was gone with the maple leaves down Hanford Road. My peace of mind had been shattered just as thoroughly as my favorite coffee mug, and I had only two short days to reassemble it.

That task was futile, but in my unglued state I at least had the sense to ask for help. I called my housekeeper and asked her to come in for an extra day. Mrs. Adams is an elderly but energetic Jamaican lady who worked for the previous owners of my house. She was happy to transfer her loyalties to me when I took up residence, and my life has been improved greatly by her talents.

When I explained that I had company on the way, Mrs. A. aired out all the rooms I seldom enter and remade all the beds. She ironed a linen tablecloth and eight matching napkins. She polished the family silver. She smiled when I burst in the door with an armload of flowers, and she helped me arrange them.

"I'm available tomorrow evening, Mr. Spencer," she said before she left on Tuesday, "if you'd like me to prepare and serve you and your guests dinner."

I noted her use of the plural with appreciation for her natural diplomacy. I had divulged nothing about who was scheduled to arrive Wednesday night, but I had no doubt that Mrs. A. had divined at least part of the truth from my adolescent awkwardness.

"Uh, no, thank you," I replied. "I—I really don't know precisely what our plans will be. But thank you, Mrs. Adams. And thank you so much for coming today. The house looks wonderful."

"Your mother would love all the flowers," Mrs. A. said as she left. As usual, she was right. Next time Mom visits, I promised myself, I'll fill the place with roses.

The only thing left to do to prepare for Olivia's arrival was to set up my fiber optic camera. The device is a dream come true for violin appraisers. Its raisin-sized camera is mounted on the end of a narrow, flexible probe. When inserted inside the sound box of an instrument, it displays images of the interior on a monitor.

Violin makers have always placed their labels inside their instruments, and although they're visible through the sound holes, they can be hard to see clearly. With my little high-tech periscope, I can look inside an instrument and see not only the label, but also construction features and other identifying marks. I plugged the camera cable into my computer and arranged the probe next to it, and with that my preparations were done.

I still had all of Wednesday to kill. If Olivia arrived at Kennedy sometime around five, she'd be stuck in rush hour traffic on the Sawmill Parkway. I figured eight o'clock was the earliest she could possibly get to my place. Would she be hungry? I didn't want it to look as though I'd made too many plans, so I stocked up on a few deli items and retrieved three bottles from my wine cellar: a white, a red, and a champagne. We might have something to celebrate, after all. The violin might be a treasure.

Teddy and Olivia together again! That was what I really wanted to celebrate. But I knew all too well that it takes two to make a reunion, and I struggled to remind myself that Olivia might want nothing more from me than professional expertise. Our relationship had been so painfully unresolved all these years that it was foolish to expect she would hold a single friendly feeling toward me. But it didn't matter what the hard truth might be. My hopes resisted all attempts to quash them.

Around nine, I drove into the village and got a haircut. Returning home, I retired to my practice room. Everything was ready for Olivia's arrival, and the only way I could spare myself an agonizing day of anticipation was to play my violin.

I lost myself in the music, and the hours drifted by. The practice room has windows on opposite sides, and the sun shifted from one to the other as morning gave way to afternoon. The first golden rays of sunset were beginning to rake across my music stand, and I had just finished the Beethoven Violin Concerto when the doorbell rang.

My doorbell rings so infrequently that I barely recognize the sound. Mrs. Adams has a key, and my mother never arrives on her own. If visitors arrive when I'm working at my computer, I see them before they get to the door. But visitors rarely arrive. I don't entertain, and this isn't a drop-in kind of neighborhood.

I set my violin down on the piano and hurried into the hall.

Chapter 37

When I opened the door, my first thought was how little Olivia had changed, not from the last time I saw her, but from when I knew her in high school. She was wearing a dark blue V-neck sweater, and a delicate gold chain disappeared in a point between her breasts. A light breeze caught her long smooth hair and blew it back from her face. She shivered a little and smiled.

"Brrr," she said. "It's a little chillier here than in L.A."

"Oh—come on in," I said, recovering as quickly as I could. Olivia walked through the door I was holding open for her and turned to face me in the hall.

"I should have called to let you know I'd be getting in earlier, Ted," she said. "I'm sorry."

"It's—it's fine, Olivia. I was just practicing."

This wasn't starting any too well, and Olivia wasn't even wearing a coat I could offer to take. The only thing she was carrying was a brand new black violin case. No purse, no suitcase. As I had feared, she only wanted a free appraisal, nothing more.

Get a grip, Ted. She's just a client.

"Well, come on in," I said awkwardly.

"Ted, your house is lovely," she replied as she followed me toward the study.

"I bought it a couple of years ago, after my father died. My mother—"

"I'm sorry about your father."

"Thanks. He went out the way he wanted, though. Heart attack on the golf course. It was all over very fast."

"How's your mom doing?"

"Pretty well. She moved to a condo in Newport Beach, and I bought this house to hold all the rest of the family stuff. She visits often. How's your mom?"

"She's fine. She loves living at the beach."

We were standing in the south end of my study. Yo Yo suddenly announced his arrival with a long, whiny yowl, and Olivia bent to pet him.

"He's beautiful, Ted."

"He's company."

We were silent again, and I watched Olivia take in her surroundings. God, she was beautiful, and even though I hadn't seen her in over ten years, she was still so tantalizingly familiar. And yet, there was something different about her, too, something deeper, a richness I longed to lose myself in.

At last she looked at me.

"I've got this violin," she said.

"I'm sorry about Arturo."

Olivia set the case on the desk in front of her. It was exactly the kind I had suggested she buy to transport the instrument safely. I switched on the light directly above it. Snapping open the catches, she lifted the cover. Inside, surrounded snugly by soft gray insulation, was a violin. Its surface was smooth and flawless, and I was pleased to see that it was perfectly strung.

"May I?"

"Of course!"

As I reached to grasp the violin by the neck, my fingers brushed one of the strings. A single, clear note rose in response to my unintentional pluck, and as I listened to its perfect sweetness, a thought burst into my mind.

Slowly I turned the instrument over in my hands, and I stared in amazement at what met my eyes.

There was no mistaking the design. There were the roses, inlaid around the back edge of the violin in place of the usual purfling. I'd seen too many drawings not to recognize them, and I'd read too many glowing descriptions. Could it be?

I expelled a breath and forced myself to remember that the likelihood this violin was the genuine article was practically nil.

"I hope this is something good, Ted," said Olivia, smiling. "I've never seen an inanimate object strike you dumb before."

"Let's take a look inside." I picked up my fiber optic camera and inserted the probe inside the violin's body.

"Watch the screen," I said, and Olivia moved closer to me as images appeared on the monitor.

It wasn't long before a label appeared in front of us. It was yellow with age, but still perfectly legible: "Joseph Guarnerius fecit Cremonae anno 1742 IHS."

I held my breath as I moved the camera slightly. The roses and the label were two out of three. Would I find the third identifying mark?

Suddenly, there it was. Burned into the wood just below the label was a coat of arms, and just below that, one word: MERINO.

This time I really was dumbstruck.

"What?" said Olivia after I had remained mute longer than she could stand. "What is it, Ted?"

I picked up the violin, and Olivia followed me as I moved to the coffee table in front of the fireplace and laid it gently down.

"Let's sit down, Olivia," I said. "I've got to tell you a story about a violin."

Chapter 38

Having a story to tell was a real blessing. It helped untie my tongue.

"Olivia, your violin was made in 1742 by Joseph Guarnerius. His name isn't as well known as Stradivarius, but many violinists prefer the stronger character and tone of his instruments, and many of them are equally valuable.

"We don't know who commissioned this particular violin, but we do know that a man named Luigi Tarisio bought it from a Benedictine monk in 1844—"

"Wait, Ted," interrupted Olivia, laying her hand on my arm. "How do you know so much about my violin—right off the top of your head?"

I looked at her for a moment before answering.

"Because every violin lover knows about this violin," I replied at last. "This violin is probably the most sought-after violin in the world. And one of the most valuable. Olivia, it's worth millions."

It was Olivia's turn to be speechless.

"Tarisio," I continued, mostly to fill the vacuum of her silence, "sold it to a wealthy Florentine aristocrat, Giuseppe Merino, who thought so highly of the instrument that he branded it with his family coat of arms." I gestured toward the computer monitor, and Olivia nodded her understanding.

"An Englishman named Phillip Kendall was the next owner. He was a wealthy textile merchant who bought the violin from the Merino family sometime around 1860. He gave the violin a name: the Merino Rose."

I turned the violin over, and Olivia ran a finger over the inlaid flowers.

"I wondered about those roses," she said. "I've never seen a violin with that kind of decoration before."

"It's somewhat unusual," I replied, "but it doesn't always mean that the instrument is a fine one. What it usually means is that someone wealthy commissioned it, but in this case, we don't know who.

"Anyway, Kendall was the man who made it famous, not only by giving it a romantic nickname, but also by lending it to the leading violinists of his day. Musicians all over Europe played the Merino Rose, including a very famous German one, Joseph Joachim."

I paused and looked at Olivia. For a split second, I was angry at the violin for being so wonderful. If it had been some ordinary instrument, we'd have been done with it by now, and talking about more important things, like being together again. But this violin had stolen center stage. It was demanding all of our attention, holding us hostage.

As if she read my mind, Olivia grabbed my hand. Gazing straight into my eyes, she said, "Oh, Teddy, it's so good to hear your voice."

Oh, Olivia. It is so good to hear yours. And to feel your hands on mine.

We sat there silent for a moment and, just as it had every time I was with her, that extraordinary electric connection arced between us. How could it still be there, after all these years and after all that had happened? I could have sat there looking at her forever, but I forced myself to continue my story.

"Joachim fell in love with the Rose the first time he played it. He spent something like fourteen years trying to persuade Kendall to sell it to him. Kendall finally relented, and on New Year's Day in 1879, Joachim played the premiere performance of the Brahms Violin Concerto on it in Leipzig. He called it 'the violin of angels.'"

"I wonder how Arturo got it—or do you know?" asked Olivia.

"Up to this moment, I don't think anybody knew he had it. The Merino Rose has been missing for well over a hundred years."

I paused, reminding myself that it was still possible that this violin was nothing more than a beautiful fake. All the right identifiers were there, and I'd heard that one pure note, but still—

"Do you want to play it, Ted?" asked Olivia, once again reading my thoughts.

"I do," I said. "In fact, I'd like nothing more. But first let me finish what I know of the rest of the story.

"About a year after the Brahms performance, the Merino Rose disappeared from Joachim's conservatory in Berlin. The thief was never caught, but one of Joachim's students, a young Italian named Vittorio Bonacci, was the leading suspect. He vanished along with the violin.

"In 1881, Bonacci died in a fire in Trieste, a big fire that killed a dozen other people and destroyed the Opera House. Rumors immediately swept the continent that the Merino Rose was also a victim of the Trieste Opera fire."

"But you don't think so?"

"Well, nobody knew for sure, and the Rose has become a kind of violin Bigfoot over the last century. Every few years, someone claims to have found it, but when the time comes for authentication, it's always a fake or nothing at all. Replicas occasionally show up at auctions, but that's all they are—copies."

"Couldn't mine be just a copy?"

"It's possible, but—"

"Now I understand," interrupted Olivia suddenly. "Now I know why Arturo left me his study. The real gift was the violin, and by hiding it in a room full of furniture, he made sure I got it."

She stopped talking, and both of us stared at the instrument between us.

"If you played it, would you know for sure?" she asked quietly.

"I think so."

"Then play it, Ted."

Chapter 39

She didn't have to say it again. Violin in hand, I led the way into my practice room. Olivia settled herself into a stuffed chair in the corner between the windows while I tuned. Then, raising my bow, I filled the room with the opening bars of the Brahms Violin Concerto.

Every hint of doubt vanished in those first exquisite strains. The Merino Rose was like a living thing in its response to my fingers and bow, and I have never felt more inextricably enmeshed with an instrument as I played. There was no "getting to know you" period. The Rose and I fell in love at first note.

I played the whole concerto before I remembered my job as host. Forcing myself to set the violin down, I turned to Olivia.

"You must be hungry or thirsty," I said. "Forgive me for not offering you something sooner."

"No, no, Ted, I'm fine," she laughed. "Hearing you play has been wonderful. I don't think you've played just for me since high school!"

I always play just for you, Olivia! I longed to say. Ever since that day in the park, I have never played for anyone else.

"But you know, I actually am kind of famished," she continued. "I just realized I haven't eaten since L.A."

Soon we were seated at my dining room table getting ready to tuck into roast beef sandwiches and potato salad. I had offered Olivia champagne, but she declined.

"I've got to drive," she said simply, and I tried to hide my disappointment as I poured two glasses of Evian water.

Mrs. Adams had placed two purple candles on the table, one on each side of a crystal vase filled with white chrysanthemums. I lit the candles before we sat down, but somehow, as I sat across from Olivia, they seemed more funereal than romantic. How could it be, I wondered as I gazed at my one true love, that our lives had never managed to intersect for more than a few fleeting moments? I love you, Olivia, I wanted to shout. *I love you!*

But all I did was bite into a roast beef sandwich.

Chapter 40

I couldn't eat much more than a mouthful. Being with Olivia and playing her violin had destroyed my appetite. I hadn't eaten anything since an early-morning bowl of Cheerios, but the only hunger I felt was a keen yearning for all the things I'd wanted in my life but never succeeded in achieving. And all those longings coalesced into one white-hot coal in the middle of my stomach. What I wanted was Olivia, and it was my fault we hadn't spent our lives together.

Now it was too late. Olivia loved Arturo. Even though he was no longer alive, she had obviously found a soul mate in him. He must have loved her dearly to bequeath her his perfect violin. *But I would have done the same!* I screamed silently to myself as I sat staring at my sandwich. Then why hadn't I? And soon she would be gone again. Soon she would be walking out my door—

"Ted, what are you thinking?" asked Olivia.

"Uh, well, just that I'm glad you came," I answered lamely.

"Me, too. It's wonderful to see you."

Silence.

"Teddy?"

I looked at her, surprised to hear her call me by my nickname.

"The violin's for you."

"What?"

"It's for you. That's why I came here. I want you to have it."

"You can't mean—"

"I mean it. You're the one who can make it sing. I certainly can't."

"But it's worth—"

"I made up my mind when I first saw it. And I'm glad it turned out to be something special—that I can give you something really wonderful."

I was too stunned to answer. Olivia pushed the plates aside, then reached across the table and took both my hands in her own.

"Teddy, I love you. I always have, and I always will. I've long since given up on the notion that we were meant to spend our lives together, but in a way, we *have* spent our lives together. You've always been with me these—how long has it been?—these thirty-three years. When I first saw that violin, shouldn't I have thought of Arturo? But I didn't. I thought of you. You're never far from my thoughts, and when the violin came along, I knew I had to tell you."

She looked down. Then, raising her face and looking me square in the eyes, she said it again.

"I love you, Teddy."

"I love you, Olivia."

It was my turn to look down.

"Screw the violin," I said.

"What?"

"To hell with it. I want you."

I looked at the candles. They were weeping now, spilling purple wax all over the linen tablecloth.

"You've always had me, Ted," said Olivia at last. "Ever since we stood side by side that day in Isla Vista Park. Do you remember? I knew I loved you then, and I kept on loving you, even though life took us on our separate paths. Then, when we met in New York, and we had those magical days together—"

"Olivia—"

"It's just the way things are, Teddy," Olivia continued before I could say another word. "Life intervened again. I had a daughter to consider. And you—"

Olivia broke off mid-sentence, then went on more quietly. "I won't deny I was angry. I couldn't understand why you wouldn't wait for me. I felt as though you abandoned me when I needed you most. Believe it or not, it was Arturo who helped me forgive you. 'You can love more than one, my treasure,' he used to tell me. 'That's what makes real life better than a fairy tale.' He was right. He loved his wife, who had died fifteen years before I met him. He loved each one of his six children, and Teddie, too. And he loved me."

We stared at each other in the flickering candlelight, and I saw two tears rise in Olivia's eyes.

"His name was Arthur," she said. "Arturo is Italian for Arthur."

Puzzled, I looked at her.

"Don't you see? You were Lancelot. I was Guenevere. He was Arthur. He's the one who noticed it, years ago when I told him about you and *Camelot*. He thought it was funny. He told me that if I forgave you, I'd grow old without wrinkles."

I smiled at that. "Looks like it's working. I swear you haven't changed since high school."

Olivia sighed and shook her head.

"I'll never know why he gave me that violin. All I'm sure of is that I want you to have it."

"Olivia—it's too much."

"It's not enough. But it's what I have to give, Teddy."

Olivia leaned toward the dying candles. Cupping her hand behind each flame, she blew them out. We sat there in the darkness for a moment, and then she rose with a sigh. Picking up our plates, she moved toward the kitchen. Not knowing what else to do, I gathered the remaining silverware and followed her.

"I should be going now, Ted." Olivia set the plates in the sink. "It's been wonderful to see you, and thanks so much for dinner."

This couldn't be happening! Olivia couldn't walk back into my life and then walk right back out again! This was our last chance! This was when it could all work out!

"Please stay," I blurted. "Please."

"I can't, Ted. I have to be back in L.A. tomorrow. My mom's got a doctor's appointment. I always take her. And Teddie's opening in *Les Misérables* on Friday."

"Olivia—"

Olivia turned toward me and put a hand on each side of my face.

"Shh, Teddy. It's time to face things for what they are, which is pretty damned wonderful. We've had the perfect love, you and I. We should thank our parents we broke up in high school, you know. We would have ended up hating each other."

"No!"

"Yes, we would have. We both wanted to be stars."

I stared at her.

"But later," I said, "when—"

"It wouldn't have worked out then, either, Ted."

"It could have, if I hadn't—"

"No. I spent a long time thinking it was your fault, but it wasn't. We were just saved again, protected from trying to live together, which would have been a disaster. But don't you see? It's meant we could keep on loving each other."

I didn't know what to say. How could it ever be a good thing that we'd led separate lives?

"You've been the beautiful music, Ted," Olivia said, "always there in the background. Always perfect."

And always unfinished, I couldn't help thinking. Always unfinished, unless—

"What about now?" I blurted suddenly. "I mean, well, here we are. We're both—we're both—" Somehow I couldn't bring myself to finish my thought. It might sound as though I was glad Arturo had died.

"Free?" Olivia read my mind easily.

"Well—yes."

God, how I wanted to gather her into my arms and never let her go.

"I really do have to go, Ted," said Olivia quietly.

"Come back."

"We'll see. I—I—we'll have to see. Ted, I'm happy now. I've got my mom and my daughter and my work, and—and two big dogs who love to walk on the beach every evening."

She gave me a look I couldn't read.

"It's funny, really. Back when I was fighting with Jay about who would get the house and the money, I felt as though I was fighting for my life. And you made me so mad when you told me to take Teddie and walk away. I couldn't do it. It just felt too important. I couldn't walk away from it any more than you could have abandoned your violin on a bus stop bench."

We both fell silent. I struggled for words that might keep Olivia with me a little longer, but no words came.

"I suppose if I had just walked away—" She shook her head. "No, no. I would have ended up hating you for making me do it. And anyway, it's pointless to think about what might have been."

Olivia departed a few minutes later, and the violin stayed behind. I entreated her one last time to take it with her, but she was adamant in her refusal.

"Play it again, Ted," she said, and we both laughed sadly at our *Casablanca* farewell. I have never felt more alone than I did as I stood at my kitchen window, watching two red taillights disappear around the bend in Hanford Road.

Chapter 41

How long I stood at the window, I can't say, but when I finally turned away, I knew it was going to be a long night. I am sometimes afflicted with insomnia, but I always have an easy solution for nocturnal restlessness. I play my violin, until sunrise if that's how long it takes for drowsiness to set in. But tonight I'd find no solace in my strings. I couldn't bring myself to play the Merino Rose, and no other violin would do.

I returned to the practice room and regarded the violin, still sitting like a rebuke on the coffee table. The King of Strings—a miracle, really—but not powerful enough to win back Olivia for me.

Reluctantly, I placed the Rose in the case Olivia had purchased for it, snapped it shut, and carried it to the walk-in vault where I store all my fine instruments. The vault is the only modification I've made to my house, a fire-proof fortress required by my insurance company. If the entire house burns to the ground, that vault will still be standing and, if the manufacturer's promises are to be trusted, whatever is locked inside it will be undamaged.

As I set the violin case on an empty shelf, I couldn't shake the feeling that the vault was too much like a mausoleum. The Merino Rose doesn't belong here, I thought, trapped and mute in temperature-controlled darkness. It's been hidden too long from a world that still remembers its excellence, still longs to hear its exquisite voice. For a moment, I was tempted to open the case. "Play it again," Olivia said just before she left, but I couldn't bear hearing that perfect music alone. Sighing, I turned off the light, swung the heavy door shut, and secured the lock.

I killed fifteen minutes looking for Yo Yo, finding him at last emerging from a narrow crevice between the linen cabinet and the broom closet in the laundry room. Yowling, he rubbed against my legs, and then disappeared up the stairs. It's time for bed, he was saying. What's keeping you?

Since sleep was not an option, I sat down at my computer. Perhaps I could search the Web for solace, or forget myself in a thousand games of solitaire. That, and a large tumbler of whiskey—but somehow a better part of me knew that anesthesia was not the answer.

I sighed and stood up. Usually, the house was dark this time of night, but earlier I had turned on every light in anticipation of Olivia's arrival. The whole place was still blazing, but all the cheery brightness only served to remind me that she was gone. Flipping switches as I went, I made my way through the living room to the den.

To please my mother, I had arranged all of my father's furniture in there—the big desk and oversized club chairs. I'd even set up his gem-faceting equipment in there, but unless she was visiting, I rarely entered the room.

I moved to the fireplace, where a wall sconce was burning. As I turned the switch on the lamp, I caught sight of a large amethyst crystal sitting on the mantelpiece. I'd seen it a thousand times, of course, but tonight it inspired a new thought.

I moved to the bookcase behind my father's desk. Scanning the shelves filled with his books, I finally saw what I was looking for.

Carefully, I pulled out the black box and set it on the desk. Sitting in my father's big chair, I unfastened the clasps and removed the lid.

The case was divided into little white satin-lined compartments, and each one held a gemstone. One by one, I turned them under the banker's light—a ruby, a sapphire, an emerald. At last, there it was, a diamond slightly tinged with pink.

"For when the right girl comes along," my father had said.

I turned the diamond over and over in my fingers.

Olivia didn't say, "Don't follow." What she said was, "We'll have to see."

I slipped the diamond into my pants pocket and flipped off the light. Yo Yo followed me upstairs, yowling all the way.

Chapter 42

The lights were on upstairs, too. I moved from room to room turning them off, arriving at last in the guest room furnished with the bed where Olivia had once slept long ago. It's even possible she slept on these same sheets, I thought as I sat down. My mother bought only the highest quality linens, and they seemed to last forever. Yo Yo jumped up next to me on the quilted silk bedspread, purring loudly and rubbing against my body. I stretched out, and the cat lay down, too. The next thing I knew, it was morning.

Morning! I couldn't believe it. I was so sure I'd be in for a sleepless night, but somehow I had slumbered like an innocent. I sat up. Yo Yo was long gone. I looked at my watch. Almost eight. I swung my legs over the side of the bed and rubbed my eyes. God. I hadn't even taken my shoes off.

Suddenly remembering, I felt in my pants pocket. I smiled. The diamond was still there. Nothing else mattered now, and I didn't bother changing my clothes before getting to work.

First, I called Mrs. Adams.

"Of course, Mr. Spencer," she said. "I'm always happy to take care of your kitty. I'll drop by every evening. Don't worry about a thing."

Next, I phoned my lawyer.

"I'm glad I caught you, Nestor," I said. "I need to change my will."
I told him about the Merino Rose and the simple bequest I had in
mind.

"That's correct," I said as he repeated my instructions. "Theodora
Conklin. Her mother's name is Olivia de la Vega."

I've just taken a quick shower, and I've thrown a few things into
a suitcase. I'm about to jump into my car and head for Kennedy
Airport. I have never traveled without reservations, never walked
up to an airline agent and said, "One ticket to Los Angeles on your
next available flight." I have never boarded a plane without a violin
case in my hand.

Olivia, you didn't say, "Don't follow." You said, "We'll have to
see."

Yes, you shall see, my dearest love. I can no longer live my life
wondering what might have been.

One More Chapter

In Los Angeles, I picked up a rental car, a white Chevrolet. It was smaller than I would have liked, but I didn't have a reservation, and nothing larger was available. I folded myself in behind the wheel and headed for Malibu. It wasn't until I was driving north on the Pacific Coast Highway that I realized I hadn't taken my overcoat off. I should stop, I told myself. I'll be more comfortable without it. But I couldn't stop. I couldn't even stay under the speed limit. I was too close to my destination, and the sun was going down.

As the ocean turned to gold, I smiled as I remembered how, on a similar evening long ago, Olivia and I had sung all the songs from *Camelot*. Pelicans skimmed along the breakers, and I could see a few diehard surfers silhouetted against the fiery sky. I couldn't help myself. I pressed my foot down on the accelerator and drove even faster.

I slowed as soon as I saw the Malibu sign. There was still enough daylight to see house numbers, and I squinted to read the addresses on the beach side of the highway. Braking near a house with a red tile roof, I swerved across the southbound lanes. A truck honked as I pulled to a stop in a parking space on a bluff overlooking the ocean. I pulled myself out of the car and slammed the door. Wind caught my big coat, billowing it out like a cape. I pulled it around myself and looked down to the strand.

The sun, huge and orange, had just reached the water. In the raking rays, I saw a woman walking on the beach below me. The wind was blowing her long dark hair. She cast a stick high into the surf. Two large dogs plunged after it into the waves.

There was no pathway down to the beach, only huge boulders. I was wearing leather-soled loafers, but I scrambled down anyway, trying to land on the ice plant growing between the rocks. I banged both shins on the way down, but at last I jumped down onto the sand.

Kicking off my shoes, I picked them up and ran stocking-footed up the beach, my coat flapping behind me. As I drew nearer, she turned to watch me. My heart thudded when I saw her face. I stopped.

"Olivia!" I bellowed, but the wind was stronger than my voice.

I rushed forward again. Now Olivia seemed to be moving, too.

"Olivia!" I yelled, still running, and ever so faintly I heard her reply.

"Teddy!"

The sun fell below the horizon as I reached her, turning the sky a deep magenta. Olivia fell into my arms, and the wind wrapped my coat around both of us. The two exuberant dogs lashed their sandy wet tails against our legs as we kissed again and again. I kissed her face, her hair. I held her to my heart.

"Olivia," I managed to say at last. "Marry me."

Olivia turned her face up to mine. She gazed at me solemnly. She touched my cheeks with her fingers. I couldn't take my eyes off hers as my heart began to pound. What was she thinking? What would she say?

All at once, her face broke into an impish grin.

"I'm really glad you're here, Teddy," she said. "You and I have a symphony to finish."

Playlists of the musical works
mentioned in *Strings* are available online at
meganedwards.com/strings

Acknowledgments

The people in this story, like the fabulous violin, never existed. I made them up. This would have been impossible were it not for the generous help and sharing of expertise I received from so many people that I cannot list them all here. To all of you, my deepest gratitude.

Thanks especially to Brian Skarstad, who showed me his studio and gave me the idea of building a story around a missing violin. Thanks to Libby Brennesholtz for making the introduction.

To Lorenz Gamma, Ming Tsu, and Andrea Bensmiller, my thanks for sharing knowledge of violins, composers, and details about the lives of musicians. To Eric Chiappinelli, Michael H. Dickman, and John Tsitouras, my gratitude for insight and inspiration, and to Jeff Tegge, my appreciation for guidance and support.

To my editors Maureen Baron and Nancy Zerbey, thanks for meticulous attention to both detail and big picture. To Jennifer Heuer, thanks for making my words look elegant and wrapping them in a beautiful cover.

Thanks to Grouchy John's Coffee for inspiring surroundings and deliciously effective caffeinated beverages.

Lastly, thanks to violinists everywhere. I can't imagine a drearier world than one without strings.

About the author

Megan Edwards is a writer and editor in Las Vegas, a city she unexpectedly fell in love with when she arrived in 1999 for what she thought would be a short visit. Life's full of surprises, though, as she had discovered seven years earlier in California, where a wildfire destroyed her home and all her worldly possessions. Seizing the opportunity sudden "stufflessness" provided her, she took a multiyear road trip on the highways and byways of North America with her husband and her dog. A former Latin teacher, Edwards has lived in Costa Rica, Italy, Germany, and Greece. This is her second novel.

OTHER TITLES BY BEN K. GREEN AVAILABLE IN
BISON BOOKS EDITIONS

Horse Tradin'
The Village Horse Doctor: West of the Pecos
Wild Cow Tales